ARTIFICIAL DIVIDE

Edited by Robert Kingett
and Randy Lacey

Cover art and design and interior design by Nathan Frechette. Edited by Cait Gordon, Nabiha Rasool, and Molly Desson.

Legal deposit, Library and Archives Canada, October 2021.

Paperback ISBN: 978-1-990086-08-3

Ebook ISBN : 978-1-990086-12-0

Audiobook ISBN : 978-1-990086-19-9

Renaissance Press - pressesrenaissancepress.ca

Printed in Gatineau

We acknowledge the support of the Canada Council for the Arts.

Conseil des Arts du Canada **Canada Council for the Arts**

To everyone with a disability
who were told they couldn't do it, but tried
anyway.

TABLE OF CONTENTS

Introduction by Robert Kingett 1

Night Pixie by Heather Meares 7

Mishipizheu by Tessa Soderberg 16

Getting Back Alive by Lawrence Gunther 22

A Time for Poppies by Ben Fulton 34

The Misty Torrent by Ann Chiappetta 68

The Glasses by Eunice Cooper-Matchett 81

Touched by an Angel by Rebecca Blaevoet 93

The Blood Trees by Jamieson Wolf 105

Noa and the Dragon by Jameyanne Fuller 122

A Firefly of Hope by Alice Eakes 149

Heroic Dreams by Randy Lacey 177

How Is It You Sing? By Niki White 184

Student Teaching by Felix Imonti 204

Catgirl, Heart and Skin by Melissa Yuan-Innes 222

Life After Dark by Anita Haas 237

Inspiration Porn Star by M. Leona Godin 269

Acknowledgements 301

About the Editors 303

About the Contributors 305

INTRODUCTION

by Robert Kingett

I remember the first out-and-proud fiction book I read that included an openly gay character. Actually, this book had gone above and beyond. It was a gay utopia for me because some of the characters are also openly trans and proud of who they are. What made this book so special to me was the fact it was a safe space before I knew what a safe space was. The book is *Boy Meets Boy* by David Levithan.

Growing up in Florida, I don't remember anyone encouraging me to read books with openly gay or bi or trans people in it. People loved the fact I loved to read, but I was never actively shown any books with LGBT+ characters and themes. I had to find those books on my own. Even after I'd found them, I had to keep them in the closet with me because I knew society didn't see them as "normal."

I just can't shake those early years of thinking I wasn't wired the way the rest of society seemed to be, just because I am not at all sexually attracted to women. I didn't understand how a book such as *The Princess Diaries* by Meg Cabot was only for girls, and why I shouldn't be reading it.

I didn't understand publishing's desire to keep telling stories about non-disabled, straight white men. I thought, *If everybody has a story, then where are the stories about people who are Black or trans or gay or disabled?*

If I take a minute to try to think of fictional characters with disabilities in books, my brain comes up with few options. I've read many great memoirs by Disabled people, ones where I felt seen and heard because they shared my struggles, but I can't say the same thing about fiction.

Boy Meets Boy by David Levithan was special to me because it was a story involving LGBT+ characters. Nobody was overcoming their gender identity the way Disabled memoirists seemed to "beat" their disabilities on every page. I was hungry for some fun stories that just happened to have Blind or visually impaired characters telling us their fictional tale of adventure or mystery.

Even in the non-fiction I've read by Blind people, they all seemed to be about overcoming the world, not just living in it while experiencing drama and or romance. The protagonist always had to overcome blindness or learn how to be blind. The characters always saw the Blind protagonist as either strange, scary, helpless, super gifted, flawless, ignorant, clumsy, or unable to function. The memoirist would have no choice but to prove them wrong about their blindness. It made me exhausted trying to find books by Disabled authors where the visually impaired protagonist just had to deal with the plot of the story, not their blindness and the plot at the same time.

As an openly gay man, I'm witnessing in real time the progress publishing is making towards telling LGBT+ stories. LGBT+ is moving away from a genre label and characters are just LGBT+, which is great. I feel honored watching that growth. As a Blind man though, I'm afraid I'm not seeing the same progress with Disabled stories.

More times than I'd like to admit, I've googled fiction books with Blind characters. The results are not promising, every time. I go to page four or five of the Google search results, hoping I'd find a golden egg somewhere, but the results are disappointing.

For one thing, a lot of books featuring visually impaired characters are written by sighted authors. While I don't necessarily have a problem with this, I keep running into stories that are inauthentically told because a sighted writer always shows a visually impaired character dictating to their phone without using a screen reader, for example.

One exception I can remember is a book called *WWW: Wake* by Robert J. Sawyer. In that book, the protagonist uses a cane properly, uses a screen reader with the keyboard for a long time on the page, and is just a smart Blind girl who is dealing with the plot.

Even though I still go back and read *WWW: Wake* occasionally, I'm hungry for more modern fiction featuring visually impaired characters. I know there are others out there just like me who are eagerly seeking books that have people like them on the page. That's where this anthology comes into play.

This anthology features blind and visually impaired authors telling their own stories. Some authors are emerging authors. Some are more established, but they all have something to show you about being low vision.

There's a wide range of writing styles, genres, and even character archetypes in this anthology. Not every story will have a happy ending. Not every protagonist will be nice. That's the point, though. This anthology compiles snapshots of blindness to show that Blind people can be witty. Blind people can be crude. Blind people can be whimsical. Blind people can be clever or brash.

Visually impaired people have to educate the sighted daily on what it's like to be visually impaired. This even happens, sometimes, because sighted people expect us to be teachers. This book might not be an instruction manual on how Blind and visually impaired people use a computer, but it will open your eyes to characters who have flaws, outsmart bullies, learn to trust their skills, and are mischievous to get what they want.

The authors in this collection are just a snippet of the talent that's cast aside for established sighted people, who really should step aside and let Disabled voices take the publishing contracts.

I hope that you, dear reader or listener, go through this anthology with the understanding that *Artificial Divide* isn't meant to take away from sighted authors trying to be allies. We desperately need allies, but we also need people willing to listen when Blind people want to tell the stories they want to tell—with grit and grace.

It might be difficult to empathize with some of these

characters. You may love every story in this collection. That's okay. It's your journey through this book. I'd like you to ponder how you feel after reading this collection. I think you'll find that even though you may be sighted or visually impaired, and even though this character would never be your friend in real life, you do have things in common, and that maybe we're not so divided after all.

Robert Kingett,
Co-editor-in-chief.

NIGHT PIXIE

by Heather Meares

CW: Grieving, loss

She is one... the only one.

As the day turns to dusk, the sky fades from orange and pink to a hazy purple that quickly darkens. Horizontal streaks of large, shadowy clouds scatter themselves as the moon, Selene, appears in all her glory. The night garden comes to life, as the crickets invite the dance to begin with their orchestral prelude. Sunflowers and poppies hug themselves tightly and bow their heads in reverence as the night bloomers awaken. Heady perfumes infuse the air with scents of jasmine, spicy honey, vanilla, and sweet chocolate. The bees and butterflies begin to disappear, but not before the changing of the guard takes place. Moths and bats arrive to take over the pollination duties and anxiously await their cue, knowing soon they will be prey and predator, battling for the same nectar and possibly for their very lives.

The moonflower gently unfolds its large, white petals and glows in the light of Selene's radiance. In the centre of the trumpet-shaped blossom, the Night Pixie is revealed. Asteria sleepily stumbles out of her poisonous, yet protective, bed, hits the ground, and quietly mumbles curses under her breath as she curls up for another moment, not quite ready to embrace the night. She rubs her eyes and slowly opens them. Moonbeams she will never see reflect in their milky, grey-blue opaqueness. If you look deep enough, you will see tiny galaxies in her eyes, but do not look too long, for she will know.

Deep indigo locks of loose curls fall from her head to below her waist in a slightly messy manner. She stands and summons a light mist of rain, which forms a barely-there, sheer tunic that surrounds her body, leaving her arms and legs exposed. Her subtle, sparkling silver wings emerge, and the night commences.

Asteria trips over the same rock she forgets about almost every night, then lazily pirouettes through the tiny rain lilies as they open to acknowledge her presence. She stops and listens for her favourite bird to greet her from above, and tries to remember where she left her cane, or as she likes to call it, "The Wandering Cane." It helps her navigate on her adventurous walks through the gardens, but sometimes has a wanderlust of its own. This morning, Mother GiGi has requested her company, so Asteria decides not to waste any more time and relies on her other senses to guide the way.

Selene has diligently watched over Asteria since the day she was left in her care many years ago. Her mother knew she was different and would never survive in the harsh sunlight of the days. Her mother also knew of her unique abilities, which could only thrive in the eventide. She was her only daughter, and her very existence depended on this sacrifice. She named her Asteria, in honor of the night goddess of oracles and falling stars, and gave her to Selene to raise and train. Remarkably, Asteria had many of the same gifts as her namesake. Oneiromancy, a gift of dream prophecy, being one of these. She awakened this evening knowing she must visit her dearest friend and mentor tonight. It must be tonight, during the very rarest of blue moons.

Since she has lost her cane, she decides to take a quick flight instead of walking, which is her normal method for this trip. She loves being close to the earth, feeling the moss and ferns tickle her ankles as she passes by. It makes her feel at one with her world to run her toes over the smooth pebbles as she walks on them. For the most part, she has gradually removed any particularly rough or jagged ones, but occasionally runs into one here or there. She collects these to remind herself that the rough patches allow her to grow. Behind her moonflower is a giant pile of rough patches. Perhaps someday she will build a sculpture, or maybe an artistic garden wall, but for now, it's just a pile of potential.

Tonight, she must fly. She must gather the courage from within and listen to all the clues to guide her on this journey. Every time Asteria flies, self-doubt tries to talk her out of it, but then she does it anyway. She does not see Selene watching her every move, but she feels the intense gravitational pull of her, redirecting a minor miscalculation now and then. She does not see the stunning iridescent blue of the dragonfly circling her and leading the way, but she hears the fast hum and buzz as she journeys with him.

Asteria giggles as she hears the silly coots below her, signaling that she is close to her destination. Their unusual sound, somewhat like a bicycle horn, makes her laugh every time she hears them, and reminds her that all creatures are proof that the universe has a giant sense of humour. The coots are little black water beings that are neither bird nor duck, having both a beak and webbed feet. She feels Selene guide her to Mother GiGi as she quirkily flits through the air. Watching Asteria find her way through her eternal darkness with such a sense of joy amuses Selene and makes her shine just a bit brighter with pleasure.

Mother GiGi honks twice and Asteria lands gently by her side, nestled deep in the reeds. The grandest of Canadian geese, with her tousled feathers that have definitely seen better days, wraps her wing around her friend to warm her. They quietly sit together for a while, feeling no words are necessary, and they gaze out over the silent pond, one seeing and one knowing. Selene paints a beautiful picture on the still water, and Mother GiGi describes every detail to Asteria. She tells her how the light frolics and shimmers, how the darkest depths of the water are brought to life by the illumination, and how one could not exist without the other. Asteria is intrigued by the juxtaposition of it all.

They decide to go for a swim to celebrate the blue moon. Asteria perches on Mother GiGi's back as they slowly and gracefully make their way to the water lilies, and Asteria jumps onto the closest one, barely making it to the lily pad. Mother GiGi grabs the stem from below the surface and carries it in her bill, pulling her fearless friend alongside as they chat and reminisce about their many adventures over the years. Both of them feel an unbreakable bond of a rare and wonderful friendship.

As they near the centre of the pond, a gentle fog blankets them with peace. They hear the owl above and the quieting of the crickets. The frogs have now taken over the nocturne, and a bat swooshes over them as it captures a moth. Asteria spontaneously feels the need to dance on the lily pad in celebration. GiGi quietly watches and smiles to herself as the midnight hour approaches. In a low and raspy voice, she says, "Be still with me." Asteria nods with respect and sits cross-legged in the middle of the beautiful red lily. After a moment, Mother GiGi lets the stem fall back into the water and says, "I love you."

"And I love you," Asteria replies.

The majestic goose glides away in solitude, towards the moon, so effortlessly that not a ripple is made. No one knows how old she is, only that she has always been here, serving them all as matriarch. As she fades into the mist, a great silence spills forth over the water and surrounding land. A brilliant light from the moonbeams fills the fog. Every creature of the night is frozen in the stillness as they watch Mother GiGi fly like she hasn't flown in years, up the moonbeams. She is magnificent and elegant. As she reaches Selene, she gently kisses her cheek and then she is gone. Tears emerge from Selene's eyes, turning into falling stars, filling the night sky with a spectacular show like none other before.

Asteria does not move for the longest time, feeling the vast emptiness surround her. All activities have ceased, waiting for Asteria's signal to resume some kind of normalcy, but she cannot do so. The snowy owl sweeps down and gently lifts her, carrying her back to Mother GiGi's nest. She covers herself in loose feathers, and falls asleep in their comfort. A family of quail surround her and diligently watch over their night pixie. Wild dreams fill her restless mind. Vivid images of Mother GiGi, who now has the face of Asteria's true mother, a periwinkle-haired pixie with the gentlest smile, float through her dreams as clearly as if she could see. There is also an awareness of an unknown being lurking on the outskirts of her garden. So many visions swirl in her head. She is not afraid. An overwhelming curiosity lights her soul on fire and sends sparklers throughout her entire body. Once again, she knows this is real, but does not understand what it all means. She drifts listlessly in and out of this dream state, and suddenly awakens to the sound of the mourning doves breaking the silence of the night. Asteria startles abruptly and panics because she must return to her moonflower before it closes. As she stands, she stumbles over the missing Wandering Cane. This makes her chuckle and say, "Thank you, Mother GiGi."

She chooses a lovely feather and puts it in her hair, behind her ear, then quickly makes her way home. She arrives at just the right moment, that magical moment between waking and sleeping, for all of nature, no matter which side it may be on. As she allows herself to breathe for a moment, the loneliness creeps in. The knowledge that she is the only one of her kind engulfs her with a heaviness she has never felt before. Tears flood down her face, covering the entire garden in a glittering morning dew as she crawls back into her trumpet bed. The petals wrap her in a tight hug as they close around her, feeling her loss, and protecting her from the coming daylight.

Upon this cue, life reverses back to day, and the night creatures disappear. They will never forget this night, nor will they forget Mother GiGi. The Night Pixie must continue to reign over the dark, and spread her magic to all those who love her, but she will always feel as if a part of her is missing.

Just outside the borders of her garden, behind a very old lilac bush, he stands, quietly watching her for the thousandth time, maybe even more, and wonders to himself if this will be the day... or perhaps night, he finds the courage to enter her world.

MISHIPIZHEU

by Tessa Soderberg

"I'm going to go to the water," Sarah said.

"Go for it," her sister, Bonnie, said. "Just be careful, it's pretty rocky."

Sarah nodded. Using her hiking stick to feel her way, she followed the sound of the waves to the water's edge. While her sister threw sticks farther up the beach for their three dogs, Sarah squatted, totally absorbed in the sounds of Lake Superior.

She couldn't see the water, but after a lifetime of questions, Bonnie had developed the skills of a landscape painter when it came to describing things. Sarah could imagine the flakes and slivers of ice tossed on slate grey water, the lapping waves, and the far-off shape of Nanabijou, the Sleeping Giant, against the sky. "Hey sis, what's the Giant doing?"

"He's giving you the finger for asking stupid questions," Bonnie called. "He's fog covered, just a shadow in the distance. There's a skin of ice out there but otherwise, he's just hibernating as always."

Sarah nodded, she had seen the Sleeping Giant once, years ago, when they'd visited the park.

Someone had gone to a great deal of trouble to create a plaster sculpture of him which she'd been allowed to run her hands over. She had been amazed by how human a peninsula of rock could seem. It saddened her that the sculpture was now locked behind glass where it could only be seen, not experienced. She could imagine him out there in the icy waters of Superior, brooding over his buried silver.

She listened to the muted crackle of new-born ice as it frizzled into nothing in the sub-freezing water. It was a soft static sound, like frying. Above it she heard the clink and clatter of glassware as more substantial bits of ice were rattled together like dishes on a badly balanced tray. Every wave created a symphony of glass, and she wished she'd brought something along to record the music.

Splash, splash, splash. Sarah jumped, then turned her head to find the origin of the sound. Splash, splash, splash. It was a swimming noise, the sound of something, someone coming. "Bonnie!" she called. "Bonnie, something's in the water."

She leapt to her feet and backed away, dropping her stick and stumbling over a boulder as she did so. On hands and knees, she scrambled away from the water's edge in sheer panic. Too many childhood evenings spent with her sisters in front of late-night television, while they described in full detail the monsters who reached out of the fog, or out from under the bed. She saw Tolkien's tentacled Watcher rising out of the depths to grab her. She smelled fish, as though something from the deep had stirred up the stink. Sarah had too much imagination not to flee.

"There's nothing there," Bonnie called, hurrying over, the dogs bounding and barking around her. "Honest Sarah, there's nothing."

"It sounded like someone swimming. You know, heavy splashes like you make doing the front crawl. I swear it sounded like someone was in the water. And the smell, I swear I smelled something."

Bonnie laughed. "The only thing in the water is water, little waves tumbling up along the beach here."

The splashes came again, and Sarah pointed silently, following their progress with her hand. "Waves," Bonnie said. "Just little waves, they come round the point in groups like that, I guess. Nothing out there at all. Besides, who in their right mind would be swimming this time of year? The bears are all in bed, and the moose have better things to do, and people, though stupid, probably aren't that stupid."

Sarah laughed. "Well, they do that polar-bear-plunge thing every year, but I guess you're right. Just waves." She patted the dogs as they brushed against her on their way to the water. She listened to the clatter of pebbles under their feet, followed by snorts, snuffles, and sneezes as they lapped at the waves. "Remember the sea monster from that book about the Edmond Fitzgerald? Maybe he's out there stirring the waters with his tail looking for lunch. Look hard, see anything sort of snake-like out there? He's like the Loch Ness monster, I think. I wonder if they're related?"

"Love among the sea monsters? You going to start a monster dating service?"

Sarah laughed and stepped cautiously toward the water. "Sure, then they can scare each other instead of scaring me."

"You don't really believe in that, do you?"

"Why not? Just because I can't see the Giant doesn't mean he's not there."

"But I can see him."

"Yeah, but how credible a witness are you? Don't forget the author of that book claims a handful of trappers, a bishop, and a ship's captain all saw the sea monster. Who knows, maybe there really is such a thing."

"And maybe tomorrow, you'll be a sketch artist just like me."

Sarah listened as Bonnie stepped closer.

"Here's your stick," Bonnie said. "Are you ready to go yet?"

"In a minute or two. I wish I'd brought my digital recorder. The ice sounds amazing, I need to record it; otherwise, no one will believe what I'm hearing."

"Okay, I'll take the mutts and run up the beach a bit. Give me a yell when you're ready to go."

Sarah listened to the jingle of dog tags as they faded into the distance. She strained her ears, but all she could hear was the soft hiss of ice and the murmur of waves on the rocky shore. She wondered if Bonnie could see her from where she had gone. She wanted to call out, to be sure she wasn't totally alone.

Splash, splash, splash, but it's only waves.

Splash, splash, splash. A heavy stink of fish, all scaly and slick, filled her nostrils.

She wasn't alone. Terror told her that. Water splashed her cheek, and she turned away. On hands and knees, she started to scramble away from the shore.

Splash, splash, something caught at her ankle and she screamed...

GETTING BACK ALIVE

by Lawrence Gunther

CW: Being blind and lost in a winter storm, ableism

It was a typical February morning when I set off for a day of ice fishing for walleye with a couple of guys I met over Facebook. The fishing was good. The company... not so much. No angler, blind or not, should ever have to go through what I experienced.

The first rule of ice fishing is never trust the ice. It's especially true when fishing on rivers that are, at best, only partially frozen. It's why I never go ice fishing alone. Hooking up with other anglers is normal because of our unwritten code to always pair up. Unlike the ice, however, a guy should be able to trust his fishing buddies.

Judging by their text messages, the two guys I'd planned a day of ice fishing with seemed all right. Neither had a vehicle of their own and were happy to take me up on my offer to use my truck. I explained I was a blind angler, as sometimes this can be a deal-breaker. It's the sort of information I never like to spring on anyone at the last minute. But for some reason these two guys never quite seemed to have grasped the concept of blind. It does happen on occasion that someone I'm just getting to know might forget, but not over-and-over again. Could it be these guys confused my being a blind angler with someone who "fishes blind"? Fishing blind is what all of us anglers do when we have no idea where to cast next. Of course, it could all be my imagination, which my wife says can be quite "lively" at times. I'll let you be the judge.

Looking back, I think the day first started going downhill when we were preparing to head on to the ice. Somehow, I ended up with the giant sled. This thing is at least twice the width of a regular gear hauler. Over hard-packed snow or bare ice, it's not a big deal as long as the load is reasonable. Add a few inches of soft snow though, and it's like pulling out a snowmobile stuck in the slush.

I understand that someone had to pull the bigger of the three sleds, but what bothered me most is the way the guys divided up the gear. I ended up with the double thermo pop-up tent, two full minnow buckets, three folding metal chairs, a propane heater, and extra propane tanks. They even tossed in the ice spud, sonar unit, and several backup lead-acid batteries. Between the two other much smaller sleds, the guys divided up the auger, three tackle bags, ice fishing rods, and seat cushions. By the time I became aware of the sled assignment and imbalance in our respective loads, the guys were already heading out of the parking lot and on to the ice. It was all I could do to catch up.

These plastic gear-haulers make quite a bit of racket when dragged over ice or hard snow, so I just follow the sound. Well, that's how it's supposed to work anyway, it doesn't work so well if you're not in earshot. I worked up quite a sweat just trying to keep up.

Our goal was to set up over water seven metres (twenty-one feet) deep, close to where the river bottom begins to rise. This meant heading away from shore and towards the open moving water in the middle of the river. Naturally, everyone knows the closer you get to open water, the thinner the ice.

Being the owner of the gas auger, the guys thought it was best if I drilled the test holes myself. I must have drilled a dozen holes in search of the perfect depth. With all the stopping and starting and hole drilling, I ended up losing my sense of direction. I had no idea which way we came from, and worse, in what direction was the open water. Based on the ice thickness measurements the guys took, we had a good twenty centimetres (eight inches) of solid ice under foot, so I knew we were safe. In total, I think we walked at least a kilometre.

I always feel a sense of growing excitement when I'm heading out to go fishing, right up until I take my first cast, or in this case, drop my line through the hole. It's the anticipation that makes all the effort and preparation worthwhile.

It wasn't long before we were all catching walleye. I caught one giant I thought for sure would win me our bet on biggest fish. But according to the guys, my fish was just a bit short of one caught and released just moments before. Normally, I like to measure my own fish using the tactile ruler on the handle of my Frabill ice scoop, but they insisted on doing all the measuring. Without the two fish to compare, I had no choice but to pay the guys twenty dollars. I know anglers are known for stretching the size of fish caught, fish that seem to grow bigger each time the story is told, but it's an unwritten rule that without proof, we never call each other out on important matters like fish size. However, there are exceptions to this rule as witnessed during professional bass fishing tournaments that now conduct polygraph tests of the top-ten winners.

The river we were fishing was known for holding giant lake sturgeon years ago. One of the guys actually hooked into one of these massive fish that they swear measured at least three metres long. They were going on and on about just how hard the fish was pulling, and seemed to be enjoying themselves immensely trying to reel it in. The guys claimed it was so big, there was no way it was going to fit through the hole in the ice. I never did get to feel the fish myself, as they managed to release it under the ice. Now, there's a time each of us are convinced that we are hooked into a true monster, only to find out that it was nothing more than a tree branch, or worse, a boot. I'm not saying these guys were deluded, so in the interest of maintaining good relations, I kept my mouth shut.

We decided not to relocate into shallower water to take advantage of the late-day bite, but instead, to head straight back to the truck. It was around then that things took a turn for the worse.

According to my weather app, the wind was now blowing steady at forty kilometres per hour directly down the river and straight into our faces. The temperature was dropping fast, and the wind chill was approaching minus twenty-eight degrees Celsius.

Taking down my double-wide pop-up ice shelter turned out to be quite the challenge. The guys had me hold the guide ropes as they unscrewed the ice anchors. Now, any ice angler familiar with using tents on ice for shelter knows it's important never to let wind get underneath the tent when removing the screws holding it to the ice. The last thing you want is to have one of these pop-up tents turned into a giant parachute. I learned the hard way that these guys were new at this. It was touch-and-go there for a bit, but I finally managed to wrestle the tent back down to the ice, but not before I was dragged about a couple dozen metres. Only then did the guys recover from the shock of what had just happened, and rallied to help squeeze the tent back into the carrying bag.

I mentioned earlier that day to the guys that I thought the weight distribution between the three sleds was unequal. Even still, by the time I finished packing up my own gear and discovered the guys had given me the same sled and load, they were already heading for the truck.

The wind was now blowing so hard, the noise generated in the hood of my parka almost drowned out all sound. Worse, fresh snow was flying, further impinging on my ability to hear.

Falling snow is like fog to the blind: it deadens sound. Fresh snow also mutes the sound of footfalls and, more importantly, the sound of sleds being dragged over the ice. Add to this the sound of strong wind buffeting my head, and it was all adding up to a total loss of my ability to hear.

You would think that I could count on the guys to look back once in a while to keep an eye on me. But there was that incident on our way out that still bugged me. A seat cushion had fallen off one of the guys' sleds. Judging by how much time it took to walk back to fetch the cushion and return, I could tell these guys weren't in the habit of looking back and checking their loads— a rookie mistake. I was starting to worry that neither of these guys were checking, and we were about to end up with one of these situations: "*Me?!* I thought *you* were checking on the blind guy..."

I'm not sure how fast the guys were walking, but despite my hustling to catch up, it wasn't long before the only sled I could hear being dragged over the fresh snow was my own. Given the strong wind and falling snow, I had no choice but to call out to the guys for verification on their location. Each time they seemed to be further away.

Not knowing which way to walk can be a bit disconcerting if you can't see, and there's no actual snowmobile or well-established trail to feel along with your feet. Adding to my challenge was the fact that my forward direction began to meander. I'm sure if you looked back at my trail in the fresh snow, it would have resembled something akin to a hunting dog flushing game birds. The extra distance I was covering due to my meandering and my having to fight wind, deepening snow, and the weight of my jumbo sled, was adding up to make my walk back to the truck more than a bit challenging.

For some reason, I began veering to the right. I don't think it had anything to do with strong winds, or the possibility that I may have a dominant left leg. In hindsight, I think it was some sort of primal survival instinct kicking in. I had to fight the urge to turn right and head to where I thought the shore was, as I knew I was still quite far from the road and parking lot. Heading to shore now would be like admitting defeat.

Not long later, I started to suspect that the strip of ice we were following between the bank and the open water was, in fact, considerably narrower than the guys had led me to believe. I kept telling myself that it was only my imagination and pushed on.

I didn't panic. Instead of my turning a hard right and heading for the shore, I drew on my extensive experience as a blind sailor. By orienting myself using the feel of the wind on my body as a reference point, I felt confident I could orient my way back to the parking lot.

To stay warm, I pulled my hat down to the tip of my nose and zipped my jacket all the way up so my collar met my hat. There was just the smallest slit to allow fresh air to enter my nose. I had pretty much eliminated any chance of frostbite, never mind snow blindness.

I have to admit, I was starting to get a bit angry with the guys for rushing back to the truck and leaving me behind on the ice. Even if they were suffering way more than me with their eyes and faces exposed to the wind, that's no excuse to leave someone behind. I eventually stopped calling out for directions. It became pointless, obviously the strong wind and distance meant they could no longer hear my shouts.

I kept walking straight into the wind using the talking compass on my iPhone and the feel of the wind on my body to keep on track. Suddenly, I felt the angle of the ice beneath my feet shift. My initial thought was that I had strayed too close to the centre of the river and was now stepping on ice that had shifted from the current. Could it be that I was now walking on rafting ice? I stopped and strained my ears to listen for the sound of moving water, or worse, ice cracking.

Not wanting to linger, I had no choice but to move forward. All my senses were strained to the max for any sound or feeling of ice shifting beneath my feet. I had my ice picks in their holders on the front of my jacket just in case I broke through. I was also wearing my flotation suit. Still, even if I wasn't going to sink and had the tools needed to extract myself from a hole, I was walking on a frozen river and would have to deal with the current. Unfortunately, every year we lose anglers who break through the ice and are swept away under the ice by the current, only to be found miles downstream in the spring after the ice has melted.

You can't imagine the relief that flooded through my mind and body when I realized I was walking on the broken and sloping ice near shore. I could also feel the tracks of others in the snow, so I knew I was in the right area. Before I knew it, I was standing in the parking lot.

The guys had wasted no time unloading their sleds into the back of the truck and getting the motor started to heat up the cab. Following the sound of the engine, I made my way over to the truck and stowed my gear, managing to slide my giant, double-wide sled into the box on top of all the other gear. I squeezed myself into the back seat alongside the guys' coats, snow pants, boots, tackle bags, fishing rods, and all the other personal gear that can get lost or damaged if stowed in the truck box with the larger, heavier items. I was squished in, but thankful for the warmth.

I barely had my door shut before the truck shot forward. The guys said they wanted to get to the beer store before it closed. I was so upset I almost told these guys off, but I still needed to get home. Will I ever go fishing with either of them again? Highly unlikely. They still owe me for gas.

I know the rule is to never go ice fishing alone. It's why I occasionally have to reach out over social media to find someone who has the same day off work and family responsibilities as I do. I would be surprised if someone doesn't invent a fishing-buddy-finder app, something along the lines of that Tinder app the guys said they were using to plan catfishing trips.

Being a blind outdoor enthusiast means taking risks. Whether I'm in my Blind Fishing Boat, on my kayak, wading a river, or fishing aboard my big boat on a stormy day, there are risks. The same goes for everyone. The difference being that most of the safety rules people go by are designed to keep sighted people safe. In many ways, I'm having to write my own rules through trial and error.

A TIME FOR POPPIES

by Ben Fulton

CW: Military, abuse of power, death and injury, PTSD

"Excuse me, are you lost?" called a lady's voice. Michael would guess she was in her late forties.

"No, not really. I mean, I know where I am; I just don't know where I'm going yet or how to get there," he admitted, trying to sound confident but running out of steam. "I've been here before but not on my own, and last year, things here were different."

"Yes, well, Union Station is always under construction. I'm amazed no one warned you."

"I usually get around by myself fairly well, except last time, there was a staircase to the right of the ticket booth over there," Michael said, waving his cane at a ticket booth about twelve feet away. "Now it's fenced off, and I'm not sure how to get around it."

"Where are you trying to go?" the lady in her late forties asked.

"I'm trying to get to the VIA Rail terminal," Michael replied.

"Do you have your ticket?" she asked.

"Yes, I have my ticket already, but I don't know how to get around this fence thing." Michael sounded slightly flabbergasted. He wanted to do this on his own, but the change in geography was interfering with that plan.

"Well, I'm headed over that way myself, would you like me to go with you?" The lady tried to sound pleasant without being patronizing.

"All right," Michael answered, accepting defeat. Then realizing he didn't want to seem ungrateful, he quickly added, "Where are you going?"

"I'm headed down to Ottawa for the big ceremony tomorrow." The lady sounded excited but also exhausted.

"Oh, really, that's where I'm going." Michael's voice carried far more exuberance. "Someone's picking me up at the station when I get to Ottawa,"

"So are you here by yourself?"

Michael stopped walking for a second. He hadn't realized he had been walking. When this lady approached him, he was standing in front of a metal grate or fence that hadn't existed last time he was in Union Station, although that had been a year ago, almost to the day. At some point in their conversation, she started moving, presumably towards the VIA Rail terminal, but Michael had no recollection of how that had occurred. Now that her question hit a nerve, it caused him to pause momentarily in his tracks.

"My mom couldn't make it this year," he stated, taking a few quick steps to close the distance between them, as the lady continued moving away from him at a steady pace. "We usually go together, but this year she had to stay and look after my grandmother."

"Okay, so how did you get here?" the lady kept walking while talking. Michael continued to follow in the hopes that she knew where she was going and was in fact taking him to the VIA Rail terminal.

"I took a bus to Islington Station and then got on the subway." There was a moment's pause. "I'm usually pretty good at getting around, but then I usually get off at St. Clair station. I haven't been here for over a year," he exaggerated slightly.

"No worries. This station is a nightmare jungle for people who *can* see," she replied, placing the emphasis on the word can. "It's always under construction, and I'm lost here half the time myself."

"Well, thanks for going with me," Michael replied, not wanting to sound ungrateful, but not wanting to seem less competent either. It was interesting the way she had started walking naturally with him, without any of the awkward arm grabbing or questions about how she should lead him, or what to say. Now it was just as though they were two strangers headed along the same path, instead of that awkward feeling Michael often got from people trying to help him out.

"Think nothing of it. Do you go to the ceremonies every year?"

"Every year since I was twelve," he replied.

"I've only been there once before." Her voice sounded wistful in that way Michael had observed when his mom's friends would talk about anything that happened more than ten years ago.

"No, we go every year, me and my mom, except not this year because my gramma's dying of cancer, so my mom had to stay behind and look after her. A friend of my dad's is picking me up when I get to Ottawa and then we'll go to the ceremonies tomorrow."

"I'm sorry to hear that about your grandmother," she said, going up a staircase. Michael heard her voice travelling up as she ascended. His cane hit the edge of the bottom stair just as the woman said, "Stairs going up."

Michael was already automatically sliding the cane

up the edge of the first stair when he heard her say those words. He quickly found the top of the staircase and followed her, saying, "Thanks."

"My grandfather was blind," she replied as if it explained everything, and for Michael, it did. He was tired of people giving him long explanations or asking him a million questions. It was difficult enough trying to get around without having to answer a million questions or being made to feel helpless.

"He was ninety-six when he died," she continued, not breaking stride as she talked. After a short pause, she said, "Leukemia." And after another pause, she said, "I think it's right through here."

Michael followed the sound of her voice easily as she continued through a hallway. Suddenly, she stopped and spoke.

"Okay, now there's a sign that says VIA Rail. Do we have to show our tickets?"

"I think so. Last year when we came this way, I remember showing someone at a desk our tickets before we boarded the train."

"Here, I think we may have to go outside first."

"I think I remember doing that last year as well."

The two of them walked outside the warmth of the

station, briefly feeling the sleet on their cheeks as they looked for the VIA Rail terminal.

"It's this way," the lady exclaimed, taking off in a particular direction. "My name is Linda, by the way."

"My name is Michael," he replied. "Pleased to meet you."

"Okay, I think it's up at the top of these stairs," Linda explained as her voice changed elevation again.

Michael followed her up the stairs, and they were quickly back inside with the accumulated sleet on their shoulders starting to melt the second they were indoors.

Linda made her way to the ticket counter with Michael in pursuit. There wasn't anyone waiting in line, so she addressed the man behind the counter.

"Excuse me, is this where I show my ticket?" she asked, clasping her purse in front of her.

"Yes, and where are we headed today?" the man behind the counter inquired with a pleasant customer service smile.

"Ottawa," Linda answered, removing her ticket from her purse.

The man behind the counter took the ticket from her, checked it over, and tore it before handing it back to her.

"The train will be leaving from Platform B at 11:15," he said, pointing towards the sign that had a huge letter B.

"Thank you," Linda answered, taking the ticket and moving a few steps away, almost in the same motion. She then waited patiently for Michael to address the attendant.

"Hi, I'm Michael Birmingham," Michael announced, stepping towards the desk.

The man behind the desk looked from Linda to Michael before answering.

"All right, Michael, where are you going today?"

"I'm also going to Ottawa." Michael did his best to make his voice sound grown-up.

"Do you have a ticket?"

"I have some I.D.," he replied, grabbing the card from his wallet. "I was told I just had to bring my I.D. here, and I wouldn't need to print a ticket."

"Not a problem." The man took the I.D. from Michael and typed a few things into his computer. Moments later, a buzzing dot matrix printer sound accompanied the man's voice as he said, "Here you go." He tore off the paper and handed it to Michael.

"Are you two travelling together?" he asked.

"Not really," Michael responded. "I mean we're both going to Ottawa, but we just met in the station."

"Okay, will you need help getting to the platform?" the man inquired.

"I don't think so," Michael addressed the VIA Rail employee. "You'll go with me up to the platform, right?" he asked Linda. As far as he could tell, she was still there waiting for him.

"Absolutely!" came her voice from just a few metres away.

"I think we're good," he said to the attendant, as he started walking in the direction where Linda waited. He tapped his cane in a wide arc, once on each side.

The attendant called after Michael, who was already more than a metre away. "Enjoy your trip. The train leaves in about fifteen minutes."

"The platform is about fifty feet away," said Linda. "There's some stairs and an elevator right next to them."

"Which do you prefer?" asked Michael.

"I'd just as soon take the elevator." Her voice had a bit more of that exhaustion that Michael had noticed earlier.

"Okay," he replied. "Let's take the elevator."

Linda continued to the elevator. When they got there, she pressed the button. They waited in silence until the elevator arrived. Linda got on first, allowing Michael to follow the sound of her footsteps. Inside the elevator, Linda turned around so she faced Michael.

"It's pretty miserable weather out there," she commented. The sleet on her jacket had completely melted, but still left a wet patch on both of her shoulders.

"Yeah, it sure is."

The doors on the other side of the elevator opened. Linda turned around again and exited from the elevator into a small, semi-sheltered area.

"Let's wait here until the train comes," she said, not wanting to venture farther from the elevator than was necessary until the train arrived.

"All right," he agreed, not wanting to get wet himself. "It should be here in about ten minutes."

The two of them stood on the platform for a while, listening to the sounds of the water dripping off the roof. It seemed like they barely had time to catch their breath when the train showed up. Michael could hear the brakes, and he could smell burning metal as it pulled into the station. There was also that ubiquitous clanging sound that seemed to accompany all trains everywhere.

"Looks like it's here early."

"No, it just takes a while for everyone to disembark," Linda replied.

"Oh, I see."

The train had stopped moving, and the doors were now open. Immediately, people started rushing out of the train, some of them carrying luggage. In no time, the train was letting people on, and Linda said to Michael, "Let's go." She took off at a brisk pace straight towards the nearest door on the train.

"Right behind you," Michael called after her in the same way he would to one of his friends. He couldn't believe how naturally he was getting along with this stranger. He usually found himself awkward around anyone and found other people acting awkwardly around him, at least at first.

They crossed the distance between the awning and the train car in no time. They were both in the train before the sleet had a chance to do more than leave a slight skiff of water on their now almost-dry shoulders. Once inside the train, they found seats and made themselves comfortable. Michael carried everything in his backpack, while Linda had a small tote on wheels. They stowed their luggage in the compartment near the entrance and then took up seats.

Again, they fell silent as the other passengers bustled about boarding the train and stowing luggage. They remained that way for some time. Slowly, the train started moving. The smooth acceleration provided some comfort, as Michael was properly on the way towards his destination. The train attendant came down the aisle, checking everyone's ticket. When the attendant got to Michael and Linda, it broke the spell of silence that had held them since they had boarded the train.

After the attendant had checked both of their tickets, Linda turned to Michael and said, "Ottawa's a long way to go for Remembrance Day."

"Yeah, I guess it is," he replied, welcoming the conversation.

"And you go every year?"

"Yeah, we go every year—me and my mom that is— except, well, not this year." He grew a little stiffer, choking up slightly.

"Why do you go all the way to Ottawa?" she asked

gently, trying to keep the conversation moving forward as reliably as the train.

"Well," he said, "it's on account of my dad, you see. He was in the war—in Afghanistan. He died over there, actually. In the first four months of conflict." Michael's voice had a somewhat mechanical quality to it, as he relayed the story he had told many times before.

"My dad had only been there for two months," Michael continued. "My mom was pregnant with me when he was over there. The thing is that he didn't know it. Mom only found out after he had left, and he was on a mission where they couldn't communicate. The jeep he was driving hit an improvised explosive device, or I.E.D., and he was killed. They think that the driver-side front tire ran over something buried. The pressure release went off as soon as the tire ran over the device, so his death would have been instant. The jeep flipped over, and two other passengers were killed. The three remaining men in the jeep made it to a nearby farmhouse and waited there for support to show up. My father was awarded a medal for valour after he died. Two of the men from that jeep had presented the medal to my mother three days before she went into labour, and that's where I come in. I never knew my dad growing up. Some of the men who knew my father had invited my mother to come to Ottawa for the laying of wreaths. So, when I was twelve, my mother thought it would be a good idea for us to go and meet some of the soldiers who had known my dad. They offered to buy us a ticket and everything. They were nice, and it turns out that one of them was living in Etobicoke not too far from us, although he's living in Gananoque now. Otherwise, he would have gone with me today. We travelled down together one year. I mean the three of us. He came with me and mom. The three of us together..." Michael tapered off.

"And now you're headed down there by yourself?"

"Well, that guy I was telling you about—who lives in Gananoque—his name is John, and he's picking me up at the station. Then we'll go to the ceremony tomorrow."

"Incredible!" Linda paused for a moment before she added, "My husband was in the war, in Afghanistan. He died five years ago now, of a heart attack. He'd been in Afghanistan just over two months himself, when the convoy he was on came under fire. The jeep he was riding in was able to partially take cover behind some boulders. They waited for the shooting to stop and then he and the five other men on that jeep drove around picking up survivors, but my husband didn't like talking about it much."

Linda paused again before she continued. "He had problems his whole life after that. He was diagnosed with PTSD. Some nights he would wake up screaming, or he would throw something against the wall. Or he wouldn't even know who I was. He struggled for years to get treatment. He went to counsellors and doctors, but the biggest tragedy was the lack of support he got from the Canadian government. He had been asked to serve over there. He wasn't even supposed to be in any fighting, and then when he got back, no one was there to fight for him. So, he created an organization for wounded civilians, and not just physically wounded civilians. He created a place where they could go and get the treatment and supports they needed. He had to fundraise hundreds of thousands of dollars over the years, but he made it his life's work and his passion. It's what kept him going. If it weren't for that, I don't know what he would have done. Maybe he would have died even sooner, but he died five years ago now, and this year they're awarding him the Order of Canada. I'm supposed to go down there and receive it on his behalf.

I haven't been to Ottawa since the first year after Dan returned from the war. They awarded him a medal for valour. He told me he felt sick to his stomach every time he thought about that medal. He tried to explain to me what it was like to be there, but he never really could."

Linda fell silent and the two of them sat for a while, listening to the soft sounds of the train moving along the track and the snippets of conversation being carried on by other passengers.

Another attendant appeared, pushing a cart loaded with snacks and beverages. Neither one of them wanted anything from the cart, so the attendant continued down the train car, leaving Linda and Michael to themselves.

"What was your grandfather like?" inquired Michael, remembering Linda's earlier comment.

"My grandfather was a war vet. He fought in World War II. That's how he lost his vision. He was too close to an explosion. Some of the dust or shrapnel was blown into his eyes with enough force to rupture the membrane. He was captured and spent almost two years as a prisoner of war. He almost died while he was over there. When he came back to Canada, he was six foot two and weighed ninety-seven pounds. You could see every one of his ribs, and his cheeks were hollow," she paused. "He also didn't like talking much about it.

"That's actually how I met my husband," she continued after another pause. "I was at a dinner event with my grandfather. We used to go to them together. Every year around Christmas, the legion would put on a dinner for the vets, and Dan was there, serving everyone at the tables. After dinner, we were socializing, and Dan and I started talking. We had a lot in common, and he invited me to the New Year's ball down at the base."

"Dan was in the cadets. He thought about a career in the military. He was going to go to military school, but then he decided to take political science courses at Ryerson instead. He thought he could do better as a diplomat, but he was also considering journalism and reporting on overseas conflicts. He had just finished his degree in 2001. He was looking for work, and he heard about a position as a cultural advisor. His past with the cadets and his focus on international politics made him the perfect candidate for the job. He was supposed to be over there in a supportive, non-combative role."

"When he got back, he tried getting treatment, but

the supports for the military weren't available to civilians, despite what he went through. So, he ended up doing it all himself. He had to fight for everything he got, and he spent most of his time fighting for all the other civilians who served overseas in positions that were supposed to be non-combative." Linda finished her story, and for some time, Michael did not know what to say. The train continued its journey east.

He broke the silence awkwardly. "Do you have any children?"

"Yes, two of them. They're both grown now. They live in Toronto."

"Yeah," replied Michael, trying to think of what next to say. "My grandfather was also in the war. Well, he was with the merchant marines. He said they never saw combat, but he said there was always the nerves. I didn't know him much before he died. My gramma was Native. She met my grandpa after the war. So, my father was half Native. Some of the guys from my Dad's company told me about how dad was always talking about his Native ancestry. He said that after Gramma had married Grandpa, she'd lost a lot of her culture."

His dad had done a lot of research into the role Indigenous people had played in every war Canada was involved in, and Michael had spent the last four years hearing about the contributions they had made to Canada's army, including the war of 1812, before Canada was even a country. His father's former comrades felt it was important that Michael understand some of what his father knew and talked about. They had taken a shine to Michael, who absorbed the influence of the men who had been closest to his father before he died. Now Michael knew more about his heritage, and he felt it was important to share it.

"Dad was really proud to be Native. They told me he was Anishinaabe. He went to the powwow in Chiefswood Park every year. That's where he met my mom. She was participating in the women's dance competition, and he noticed her doing the jingle dress dance. She was from the Mohawk Nation of Kanesatake. They had only been seeing each other for a few months before he'd left for Afghanistan.

"Dad wanted to live on reserve at some point, but Gramma had lost her status when she married Grandpa. Dad said he wanted to get it back, but it would take some paperwork. Gramma said she didn't want to make a fuss about it. She was happy living where she was. So, it was something that never happened."

"Is that something you would be interested in?" Linda asked, curious about this part of Canadian politics that she was ashamed to admit she did not know very much about.

"I have status through my mother," Michael answered her politely. "We could live on reserve if we wanted to, but both my mother's parents are gone, and my gramma is the only one left. Mom likes being close to Gramma, and she doesn't want to change her job."

"Oh, what does your mother do?" Linda prompted, encouraging the flow of small talk as the train made a short stop in Kingston.

He responded as the flow of passengers switched from those leaving the train to those boarding the train. "She's a personal care support worker for Sunrise. It's a retirement home."

For some time, the two of them observed the bustle of activity. Neither one of them spoke as the train started moving again. They were both content to let the journey proceed for awhile without filling every minute with conversation. When the train announced the stop for Gananoque, something occurred to Linda.

"Didn't you say the person picking you up lives in Gananoque?'

"Oh, you mean John. Yeah, he lives in Gananoque now," Michael said, not yet connecting the dots.

"So, why didn't he pick you up here then?"

"Oh!" Michael suddenly caught her drift and then launched into an explanation of the logistics. "The timing wasn't going to work out. He had a bunch of things to do today, and we wanted to be there early for tomorrow. We'll be staying at a friend of John's, so we can be there early tomorrow. It just worked out for John to pick me up at the station. Otherwise, John's friend, Fred, could have done it."

"Oh, okay." Linda accepted his explanation of events. The train pulled into Gananoque, and the now familiar pattern of unloading old passengers and then loading new ones repeated itself.

In fairly short time, the train resumed its steady journey eastward. After some time, just as the silence started feeling less comfortable, Linda turned to Michael and asked, "And what about you? What do you want to do?"

"After I finish school? I'm not really sure yet. I'm thinking about maybe taking up archery, or maybe photography."

His voice now carried a lilt of mirth that encouraged

Linda to laugh.

"Ah, I see you have a sense of humour. Did you hear the one about the blind man in the beer store with his guide dog?" Linda fondly remembered her grandfather's sense of humour and his insistence that you had to laugh about things to make the world a better place. She could still hear him saying, "If you don't laugh, you'll spend all your time crying."

"No, I don't think I have heard that one before," Michael responded, now anticipating a fresh joke he could share with his friends. Most adults he met were awkward when it came to him being blind.

"Here goes," she began. "So, the man goes in with his guide dog and starts swinging it around by the tail. Then the manager comes over and says, 'Excuse me sir, can I help you with anything?' And the man replies, 'No thanks, I'm just looking.'"

Now the two of them were both laughing, and Michael could only remember one other blind joke.

"Do you know why blind people don't skydive?" he asked.

"No."

"Because the guide dogs can't stand it."

When she finished laughing, Linda turned to Michael

and asked, "Have you ever thought about getting a dog?"

"You have to be sixteen years old to get a dog. I'll be sixteen next year, so I can get a dog then, but there's a two-year waiting list in Canada. So, unless I go down to the States to get one, I'll most likely be finished high school before I have one. Mom thinks that might be a good thing, though. She says having a dog while I'm still in school would be too much of a distraction."

"So, you do want a dog?"

"Absolutely. As soon as I can apply, I'm going to. The school's in Ottawa. I have to go down there for a month to train with the new dog before they'll let me have it."

"Oh really." Linda didn't know anything about guide dogs. It wasn't something that had ever interested her grandfather.

"Yeah," Michael went on. "They have to make sure that everything is working out between the dog and the handler. They say that it's a team, and not every dog will work with everybody. Most of the dogs that start don't make it through the program. It takes them two years to train them and then they spend a month with the owner. It takes a lot to train the dogs and the owners need to learn how to look after the dogs and everything."

"So, what happened to your vision?" Linda ventured, now that the subject of blindness was being thoroughly canvassed.

"I was just born with this weird condition. I could never see very well, then I lost it altogether. It's something called retinitis pigmentosa, and I had a rapid onset. It's supposed to be genetic, but no one in my family has it. They did some genetic testing, but they couldn't find anything. They think it might be from a family member who's no longer living, like maybe my grandpa on my dad's side or something like that. They don't really know. They say it can be recessive and then suddenly mutate. They keep studying it, trying to learn more or find some cure, but all I get from the visits to the optometrist is a stinging sensation in my eyes from the drops they use to dilate my pupils, so they can photograph my retina."

"I remember getting those drops once. I have astigmatism, and they wanted to see if there was something else. They warned me that I wouldn't be able to drive afterwards, but I had no idea I couldn't function for the rest of the day. I booked the test during my lunch hour, and I couldn't go back to work afterwards. I couldn't even see to use my phone, and this was before you could talk to your phone, so I couldn't call anybody. I had to have my husband come and get me. I was so embarrassed. I can't imagine going through that more than once."

"Every six months," Michael piped up in that cheerful way that reminded her of her grandfather. Linda could not help but to admire Michael for smiling at her while he accepted the frequency of a process she could only describe as torture.

"That's horrible!"

"Story of my life."

The train started slowing down. The announcement that they would be pulling into Ottawa had already been made, but they hadn't paid much attention to it. Now that they were approaching their destination, Linda asked Michael, "Will John be meeting you on the platform?"

"That's the plan."

The train stopped. The pair rose from their seats and reclaimed their luggage. Linda helped Michael find his backpack, which had been moved by other passengers in the constant shuffling that occurred at every stop. Michael placed his pack squarely on both shoulders.

"Ready?" asked Linda.

"Yes."

"Okay, follow me."

Linda walked down the stairs onto the platform with Michael right behind her. She paused for a while, looking around to see if she could find anyone who resembled the person Michael described.

"What does he look like?" Linda asked.

"He'd be about your age. He's about my height. I think he's going bald, and he has a beard."

"Do you know what colour his beard is?"

"I think it's brown, but it might be black or grey."

John, who was waiting on the platform for Michael to arrive, noticed Michael first. The white cane did make Michael stand out a little bit.

"Michael!" he called, abruptly changing his trajectory. An instant later, he noticed the woman standing next to Michael. He would have recognized that face anywhere, whether it had been six years or sixty since he had last seen it.

"Linda!" he shouted. "Linda Blimpkin."

Linda's head snapped over immediately. "John

Simpson, is that you?"

She tilted her tote upright. Letting go of the handle, she embraced him for a moment.

"I haven't seen you since Dan passed away," John intoned.

"After the service and everything, I didn't see many of the people John worked with. Everyone was nice about it, but I just found it too painful to be around. Too many memories."

"I'm sorry," John offered.

"It's okay, I'm over the worst of it now. I've met a few of his friends and co-workers over the years. I just never felt like reaching out." Linda paused. "Someone told me you had moved out west. I just met Michael here at Union Station. When he told me someone named John was picking him up from the station, I never thought... I mean, I never would have guessed in a million years." Linda's eyes widened in dawning realization as her head shifted from John to Michael and back again. Her mouth hung open.

"Michael," John gathered his composure. "Linda's husband rescued me and the other survivors from the Jeep your father was driving. When the three of us were in that farmhouse waiting to be rescued, it was Dan who showed up to rescue us. We were never happier to see anyone else in our entire lives. When we got back from the war, we all agreed to stay together. We all worked on the Association of Severely Wounded Canadian Civilians and Vets together. Dan passed away the year before you and your mother came down to see us. We never really told you much about him, but somehow you and Linda made it down here together."

John let those words sink in. Then he turned to Linda and said, "I take it you're here for the ceremonies tomorrow?"

Linda sighed. "Yes, they're awarding Dan with the Order of Canada, and I'm supposed to receive it for him."

"So, what are you doing tonight?"

"I'm probably just going to check in to the hotel and get an early night before tomorrow." Linda's voice sounded tired once again.

"Why don't you come over for dinner? Fred's making his famous gumbo. I'm sure he'd love to see you. I know you've got to eat something, and afterward, I can drive you to the hotel."

John's enthusiasm was infectious, and Linda could not deny his logic. Also, she didn't really want to be alone; the offer of company and a warm meal sounded better than takeout in a hotel by herself. She accepted his offer, and the three of them left the platform together. John caught Linda up with what he and Fred had been doing over the last five years, throwing in tidbits about other people they both knew.

John's car was warm inside. The weather here was slightly warmer than Toronto, but not by much. It was raining. The warmth of the car embraced them as their conversation sped them toward Fred's house, twenty minutes away.

Over dinner, John and Fred filled Michael in on everything he wanted to know about the Severely Wounded Canadian Civilians and Vets. They explained why Dan had put the civilians first in the name, but why he had included the vets as well. They explained about the fundraising and the work that Dan had done with all the men Michael's father had served with. Linda finished three bowls of Fred's gumbo. She hadn't heard these stories in several years, and it was good to hear them again and remember the men her husband had rescued, both in Afghanistan, but also at home. Men her husband rescued from the same anguish she herself had witnessed.

Around 10:00 p.m., Linda looked up, declaring what a wonderful time it had been and how much she enjoyed catching up with them, but that it was also a big day tomorrow and she really should be heading off.

John's eyes caught the clock on the wall. It had been a pleasant conversation, but there was no denying the time. "All right then, I guess I should drive you home?"

John rose to his feet as Linda replied, "Oh, there's no need. I can take a cab."

"Nonsense," he argued. "I made an offer, and I'm sticking to it. Besides, you'll never get a cab to show up at this time."

John was already halfway to the door and pulling on his coat. Linda couldn't resist, so she graciously accepted his offer. Fred helped Michael get settled, showing him where his bed was and then pointing out the night light before realizing that Michael wouldn't need it. The two of them shared a laugh about that. Fred had known Michael for three years now, and he still made mistakes like that.

Michael brushed his teeth, washed his face, and put on his pyjamas. He was already in bed when he heard John return. He heard him come in and say to Fred, "I invited Linda to have lunch with us down at the Legion tomorrow after the laying of wreaths."

"What did she say?"

"She said she'd think about it."

"Do you think she'll come?"

"I'm not sure, I hope so."

Michael drifted off to sleep. He was sure there had been more conversation, but the next morning that was all he could remember. He wondered if Linda would be there again. Would they be on the same train on the way back to Toronto? That thought just occurred to him. He hadn't thought to ask yesterday.

After a quick breakfast of milk and cereal, Michael put on his jacket and tie. Two years ago, John had taught him how to put it on himself. The two of them had gone to the Value Village, and John had helped him pick out a suit. It was getting a little short in the sleeve, and if Michael continued to grow at the same rate, he would need a new one within a year. He then joined the two men in the living room, both in uniform. John drove them toward the Legion where everyone was meeting up. John and Fred were joining the parade to march to the National War Memorial. Michael was not in the parade. He would be waiting at the memorial where he would meet up with John and Fred before the three of them returned to the Legion. John dropped Michael off as close to the memorial as they could drive. Fred walked him to the spot where Michael was supposed to wait. Then he hurried back to John's car and they drove off.

Michael stood there in the chilly November air. He would be standing there for the next two hours, listening to the noises of people bustling about, hearing the parade approaching, and listening to the speeches being given. He was there when they awarded the Order of Canada to Linda on behalf of her late husband. Following the laying of wreaths, John and Fred went over to where Michael patiently waited.

"Come on," John said. "Do you want to lay your poppy?"

"Yeah," he replied. The three of them went towards the memorial and laid down their poppies together. Linda was still there. She could see them from a distance. She had noticed Michael earlier when she was receiving the medal, and she had not taken her eyes from him since. When she saw him leaning over to set down his poppy next to John's, a thought suddenly occurred to her. She hadn't fully made up her mind about whether she would take John up on his offer to have lunch down at the Legion, but that is where she was now going. She had only been there once before, so she relied mostly on her phone's GPS to get her there.

When she arrived at the Legion, several people who recognized her from when Dan was still alive and some people who only knew her from seeing her receive the award that morning were eager to congratulate her. She fumbled her way through the various thank you's and reminiscences, looking around for Michael.

One of the men who served with Dan recognized Linda and grabbed her by the arm.

"Linda, how are you? John said you might be here. We have a spot at a table for you. Come right this way."

Linda was swept along by George and an inexorable flow of traffic that directed her to a table in one corner of the Legion where Michael was seated with John and Fred sitting next to him. Before she knew it, Linda was drinking coffee and talking to men she had not seen in over five years. Linda was treated to a plate of sandwiches. No one would allow her to get anything herself or move from the table. Finally, things started wrapping up, and people were filing out and making dinner plans. Linda's train was leaving at 4:00 p.m. and

Michael was leaving the next day. They would not be travelling back together after all.

Before she left, Linda went over close to Michael.

"Here Michael, I want you to have this." She put the medal in his hand. "I think Dan would want you to have it."

Michael was speechless as he accepted the medal.

"Now I must get going or I'll miss my train, but if you ever need anything you can always call me. I made sure John has my number. I think if your father could see you now, he would be proud."

"Thank you," was all he could manage. He couldn't believe it. This was the highest award of Canada. He had no idea what his father would be thinking at that point.

Linda left Michael holding the medal, feeling the coldness of its edges against his thumb. In that moment, Michael did not know exactly what he wanted to do. He felt the weight of the honour and knew that it was up to him to live up to it.

Would he decide to live on reserve to live out his father's dream? Would he follow in his footsteps and join the army? Would he practice medicine, the way his mother wanted him to? Would he go in a new direction altogether? Michael did not have answers to any of those questions, but he knew he had to make the award in his hand mean something. Michael made up his mind right then and there that someday he would earn the Order of Canada for himself to make his father proud

One day, Michael did just that.

THE MISTY TORRENT

by Ann Chiappetta

Anita entered the hotel room, yellow Lab Riley at her heel. She held the door open for the dog to step clear before it closed.

"Riley's done his business. Ready to go?" she asked Mel, already feeling excited. It had been a long time since her first visit to Niagara and Ontario.

"Yup," Mel said. "Our tickets will be waiting at the booth."

The women left the room and walked to the front of the hotel, Riley leading the way. Anita couldn't help being proud of the guide dog; he was enjoying working in such a welcoming city.

Fifteen minutes later, the threesome exited the hotel shuttle van, and Mel and Anita made their way to the ferry boat line, Riley in the lead. They joined the line and shuffled along with the other tourists.

"It's a full moon," said Mel. "It's really big and bright."

Anita smiled, feeling the ebb and flow. It was hard to tell even her best friend of over twenty-five years that despite being blind, she already knew the moon was full and the tide was coming in, and it made her skin tingle. Mel knew Anita was clairvoyant but didn't ask much about it. That was fine with Anita; she didn't want to seem like a freak.

"I'm so glad we decided to go on this ride," Anita said. "The fireworks will be really fun."

They fell into one of their conversations about the surroundings, the people, and other observations of long-time companions and soon found themselves at the front of the ticket line. Mel got the tickets and helped Anita clear the ticket booth. They had perfected a system to help Riley guide Anita through crowds and unfamiliar places. Mel walked a few steps ahead. Anita pointed to her and gave Riley the command to "Follow Mel," and soon they were all walking with the others toward the archway leading to the upper quay. Riley stopped in the line for the elevator. The trio entered on the second trip, exited, and fell in with the crowd at the lower quay. It was much more confusing there, with small groups of tourists peppering the waiting area. Mel offered Anita an elbow, and Anita heeled Riley until they moved through the crowd to the end of the line.

Mel chuckled. "I think Riley is looking up at the

moon."

Anita nodded, wondering what he could be looking at.

"He's never done that before," she said.

Two twenty-somethings joined in behind them. Anita thought she heard bells tinkling, the kind she often heard at Renaissance fairs. It must be a new thing, she thought, to wear the silver bells for jewelry. The two girls sounded young, and one giggled at the other's words.

"There's a couple with a kid in a wheelchair. She's got a trach tube." Mel was a pediatric nurse and noticed things like that.

The couple said hello and asked Mel where they were from. The tourists said they were from Ireland. They chatted, and Anita asked if the girl would like to meet Riley. Anita often visited clients in critical care units, and Riley was a calm canine ambassador. He sat by the wheelchair and placed a paw on the girl's lap. The mother leaned forward and put a hand on his head.

"What a gentle soul," she cooed to the yellow Labrador. Anita was about to remove the paw, but the mother said it was good for her daughter to interact with Riley.

The line didn't move even after the chat fizzled out, and Riley put his paw down, returning to Anita's side.

"I sure hope it's worth the wait," Mel said, and as if her wish was heard, the ferry gangway gate opened, and the passengers boarded.

Mel and Anita posed for a final selfie on the way down the quay. Anita heard a dismayed sound behind them, accompanied by those tiny bells, and assumed the twenty-somethings didn't want to be photo bombing. She turned to say something to them, but they were gone.

"Hey, I think you scared off those kids when you took out your phone."

Mel frowned. "Really? What kids? Oh, we're next."

Before Anita could ask her what she meant, they were swept up in the line. Riley led Anita up the gangway, and someone handed her two ponchos.

"One for you and one for your dog," the ferry worker said.

Anita asked the ferry worker for the best place to stand.

"If you don't mind getting wet, to the left or right of the bow."

Anita turned to Mel. "That's where we want to be.

It'll be awesome."

Anita's grin made Mel laugh, and she helped Anita and Riley find a spot along the crowded railing at the front of the ferry. Anita felt the breeze against her skin, smelled the musty water mixed with the heady scent of flowers and something resembling sulfur. She was admittedly more than a little distracted by it. She inhaled the layered scents, which seemed to linger over her skin, and listened to the low hum of the voices of the passengers, the lapping of the water, and the faint tinkle of bells. The falls could be heard in the distance.

"Mel, are those kids back, standing to our left?"

"Oh, yes, at the bow. How the heck did you know that?"

"I can hear them." She almost said she could hear the bells, but didn't.

"Better tie down your poncho or it will whip around you in the wind," Anita said and demonstrated to Mel how to do it. She didn't bother with Riley's poncho. The Labrador barely tolerated his raincoat.

Ten minutes later, the ferry drifted away from the dock and idled toward the falls. It began to turn into the curve of the horseshoe, the power and roar of the falls crushing out all other sound. Mel and Anita stood together; each gripped the rail for support. Mel tried yelling something to Anita, but the words were ripped away by the wind as soon as they left her mouth. Anita felt the unrestrained power of the falls, the cold spray making her flinch. The ferry rocked as if in a tug-of-war, engines vibrating the deck.

Anita heard the kids to her left singing, the bells becoming shrill and pitched so high, it hurt her ears. Riley whined. The ferry jerked, then began moving backwards into the falls. Anita was overcome with a flash of terrifying clarity; she and Riley and Mel were going to be hurled to bits and pulverized on the rocks, along with the entire ferry. The next second they were floating in calm water, the falls behind them, the crushing intensity of the water muffled.

Mel's eyes flew open, and her chest filled with air, but her scream didn't come. Anita let out a breath. Fear was everywhere on their faces. Riley whined and lay on the floor, head between paws.

"What is going on?" Mel asked. "What the hell just happened?"

Anita heard the panic in Mel's voice and swallowed. Although strange things happened to Anita quite often, this was the first time it was so obvious and involved

Mel.

"Are those two girls still at the bow singing?" Anita asked.

Mel looked around. "Oh my God, Anita, we're the only ones moving!" Her grip on Anita's arm tightened painfully.

Anita's intuition took over. "Don't move. Don't ask me why, just stay put and tell me what's happening. But whisper as softly as you can, okay?"

Mel pushed out a breath. "Okay, no problem," she said, her voice oddly strained to Anita's ears, like it was a huge problem. "Those kids and a few other ferry workers are doing something, like making signs in the air."

"I think they're summoning something."

"Summoning something?" Mel squeaked. "Jesus, Anita, this isn't real, is it?" She sounded like she was on the verge of freaking out.

"I know it's bizarre, but keep holding on to me, and no matter what happens, don't let go."

Anita bent down to pet Riley, who was trembling but quiet. She held his leash even tighter. The tingle down her spine became an intense itch. Something was going to happen.

"Um, the boat is drifting toward the rock wall," Mel said.

Anita felt her ears pop.

Mel took in a sharp breath. "Holy crap, Anita, there's this huge black hole opening in the wall, and we're headed for it!"

"Close your eyes, Mel," Anita said, taking the advice of the tiny whispers that only moments before had begun flitting from ear to ear. "It's safer that way."

"Safer? Anita, what's happening?"

Anita stepped closer to Mel, found her friend's face, and shut Mel's lids with a fingertip. "Don't let go," she said, and put an arm around Mel's waist, hugging her close. Mel hugged back, tucking Anita's shorter body into hers in a protective stance.

The pressure was painful in Anita's ears, and for the span of a breath, nothing happened. In the next breath, the pain was gone, and the ferry shot forward. The falls parted like a curtain, and Anita thought she heard bells amid the mighty roar. Riley barked. The two friends were still hugging.

"It's okay, Mel." Anita felt her friend trembling and held her hand. "It's okay. It's over."

Riley pulled at his leash, sniffed the deck floor by the

bow of the ferry, and grumbled. The other passengers were laughing and feeling the adrenaline the proximity to the falls invoked. Mel and Anita stood at the railing, neither woman ready to talk about what they had just experienced or how those young people who had been chanting had disappeared. The two women were not talking excitedly or watching the torrent of water with awe like the other passengers. They were both quiet for the rest of the ride. The fireworks made them both flinch, and even Riley sighed when the short show concluded.

The ferry moved slowly back to the quay. Anita was still mulling over the implications of the wild ride through the middle of the falls when a soft, Irish-accented female voice said something to her.

"Thank you for being so kind to our daughter."

Anita, caught off guard and still reeling from the encounter, just nodded.

"We didn't think a gifted one such as you would be with us today."

Anita kept quiet, shocked to be referred to as a clairvoyant by someone other than herself. She was often told her talent was a gift, but she wasn't sold on the title. There were times, like now, when she felt it was more a burden than a boon. She had to explain things to Mel, who was most definitely a scientific thinker and non-believer.

"We don't often get the opportunity to guide others like us through the veil. I hope our little excursion didn't upset you or your companions overly much."

Anita blinked and thought, *Veil?*

"Um, no, I found it interesting," she said, thinking back to the moment of sheer terror prior to the parting of the falls and the side bar into the veil-puncture, which had freaked out not just her, but her best friend and her guide dog. She wasn't going to share that little piece of information with the otherworldly being who had most likely contributed to such a trip.

The woman might have smiled, but it was lost on Anita. "Well then, goodbye," the woman said and walked away.

Mel came up. "Anita, where were you? We're getting off now."

"What do you mean? I didn't go anywhere."

Her friend sounded confused and upset.

"Mel, what's wrong?"

"Nothing. Let's go. It's a long walk back up to the street level, and besides, I want to go into the gift shop."

Later, while the two women sipped drinks at the hotel bar, Anita prompted Mel to say what had been bothering her since the ferry ride—which, in itself, had been like a bizarre fantasy movie.

"You know that couple with the kid in the wheelchair?"

Anita nodded.

"I could have sworn she had a trach tube, and she was non-verbal. Isn't that what the dad said?"

Anita nodded again, letting the sharp bubbles of the vodka and club soda roll across her tongue.

Mel sipped a bourbon and club soda on the rocks. "Well, after that acid trip of a ride," she said, "I saw them again. Dad was fine, but the kid, she was different. Her trach tube was gone, and she was moving like she wasn't paralyzed. I thought the dad said she wasn't able to move her head, neck, or arms."

After a moment or two, Anita reached for Mel's hand. "Listen, what you saw is what they wanted you to see, Mel. Those people wanted you and everyone else to see the kid like that before being sucked into that fey place."

"Fey place?"

Anita took a bigger sip, hoping for liquid courage. "Yes, it's another term for fairy folk."

Mel took another sip of her drink and sighed. Anita knew that sigh; it was the one that meant, *Oh, no, here come the paranormal and ghosties.*

"The point is," Anita said, "we won't ever be able to make sense of what happened, because it's beyond us to understand."

The expected words of disbelief didn't come from Mel's lips. "I just want to forget it ever happened." She sighed again and ordered another drink.

The late-night dinner at the bar was quiet, and the companions returned to their room for the night. Mel had already fallen asleep on her bed. The moon peeked in through the hotel room's drapes, calling to Anita; it was odd that sometimes her ruined eyes could still tell when the moon was out. Anita slid one side of the drapes open, the familiar, cool light ghosting over her skin. She heard the faint tinkle of bells, and despite the bizarre ferry boat tour, she smiled.

She had promised Mel a great time in Ontario. They had already visited the vineyards, Niagara on the Lake for gelato, the casino, and a few memorable restaurants. She sighed because the unexplained part of the ferry boat ride would soon be lost to Mel. That's how the fey protected themselves when interacting with the non-fey. The side bar trip behind the falls would soon fade, and only the conventional ferry trip would be remembered. She would need to be careful about not sharing the "gifts" of her own memories.

A month from now, Mel wouldn't even remember it. *Maybe this is a good thing*, Anita thought, turning and closing the drapes. The tinkle of a bell sounded again, and she frowned.

She sat on the bed where Riley lay sprawled out, fast asleep. She ran her hand over his collar and found a tiny round bell on it next to his ID tag. She fingered the small, nut-sized object and grinned, bent over, and kissed the dog's head. She slipped into bed and fell asleep.

THE GLASSES

by Eunice Cooper-Matchett

CW: Internalized and external ableism, parental abuse

I was in grade one. The warm, afternoon sunbeams streamed through our one-room schoolhouse's large side windows, drawing me into my magical land of make-believe. It was a wonderful world, a world where I could see, and nobody laughed at me. In this world, I rode my white Arabian horse across the open fields, the wind blowing in my face, sending my hair into a wheat-brown stream behind my head. I opened my mouth, sucking in the cool, freeing air.

A car door slammed, yanking me out of my dream. Cold fear swept through me, leaving me shaking like a leaf. The only person who owned a car and would come to school was the public health nurse. And she was going to find out my eyes were broken.

Heavy footsteps came up the stairs, followed by the door opening. My horror materialized. Nurse Green strode into our classroom, her black coat buttoned tightly about her, and an old black, leather bag in her hand. She nodded briskly, strode to the back of the room, and dropped her bag and coat onto an empty table. Then, she hung a white square on the back wall. "Starting with grade nine," she told us. "I want you to come back, one at a time."

I watched. When nobody had trouble reading the letters on the white square, I relaxed a bit. Maybe I'll be able to see them after all.

I glanced across the aisle as Susan, a grade fiver, slid into her desk. She poked Carol in the back. "She'll never see it."

My face burned and my heart pounded. All I wanted to do was run. She was right. I would never be able to see it, and everyone was going to laugh. I looked toward the door, wondering if I could get out without being seen.

"The first letter is E," my older sister, Pat, whispered, sliding into her desk in front of me.

"Judith."

I jumped at the sound of my name. It was my turn. My stomach tightened, and I almost threw up. Even if I couldn't see them, I felt everyone looking at me, and my face burned hotter. Why didn't I run when I had the chance? Not knowing what else to do, I slid out of my desk and walked to the back of the room. Snickers came from all around me, but I kept on going.

"Over here, dear," the nurse said.

I stood beside her, searching for the E on the white square, but it wasn't there, only fuzzy black blotches. I closed my eyes tight, opening them a crack, but the black blotches remained black blotches. I began to shake. The room grew smaller. Everything in it tilted and swirled. My skin burned, as if the sun had been turned upside down and poured over me.

"It's all my fault," I sobbed, crumpling to the floor, biting my arm so hard, I left indents of my teeth in my skin. "I broke my eyes."

Nurse Green knelt beside me. "What's happening here?"

I hid my face behind my other arm. "I'm not stupid. Please don't send me away. Mommy and Daddy tell everybody I'm just wanting attention, but I don't know what that means."

Our teacher, Miss Hall, came to us, and the nurse stood up, leaving me alone on the cold wood floor. I heard them talking about a city a long way away and something that helped blind people. I bit my arm harder as I listened, trying to figure out what they really meant.

"I've talked with her parents," my teacher informed the nurse. "They think it's a game."

Nurse Green bristled. I felt it all the way down to the floor and pulled my knees closer to my chin. "Children don't play games like this." She helped me up and sent me back to my desk, where I watched her pack up her bag and then stride out of the room.

What felt like hours later, Pat and I ran into our house. "We're home," I announced to anyone who might hear me. I hung my jacket on a hanger behind the door and went to the living room. Mom sat in the chair by the heater. My little brother snuggled onto her lap, holding the book she was reading to him.

She glanced up. "You'll get your clothes changed, and the wood packed right away, if you know what's good for you." Without another word, she returned to the colourful pages of our *Big, Big Story Book*. Pat and I, like frightened mice, scurried to our room.

"I'm scared," I sobbed, plopping on the bed. "Nurse Green has been here. That's why she's mad."

"Stop it." Pat grabbed her everyday clothes and tossed me mine. "Fretting won't help, but packing the wood might."

The sun was set. Our arms ached, but the big pile of

chopped wood was almost in the wood box. "Last load," said Pat, grabbing the last piece from beside the chopping block. "Race you to the house."

"Will not."

The barnyard gate slammed, and Daddy strode up the path to the house. My arms went limp, and my armful of wood crashed to the ground. Something hot ran down my legs.

Pat looked at my soaked jeans and her eyes widened. She pushed me toward the summer house. "Run. I'll come back for yours."

Inside the summer house, I yanked off my jeans and ripped pages from the Simpson Sears Catalogue and rubbed the wet spot. "Dear God," I begged, "please make it dry."

"Judith," Mom called from the back step. "Supper."

I threw the rumpled pages down the hole. Ugly black streaks on the wet part of my jeans stared back at me. I tried to rub them off with my hands, but they wouldn't go away.

"Judith. Now—or I'll give you something you won't want for dilly-dallying."

I pulled the jeans back on and ran to the house.

Mom set a bowl of potatoes on the table as I rushed

through the door. "Get washed and up to the table."

Keeping my back to the wall, I washed. When nobody was looking, I dashed across the room, and onto my chair. I tried to eat, but my food stuck to the roof of my mouth.

Mom banged her fork on my plate. "Get busy. Many kids would be good and thankful for what you're turning your nose up at."

Daddy closed the book he was reading while he ate. I could feel him looking at me, and I began to shake.

"You're going to town tomorrow," he said. "The optometrist is in, and we're going to get to the bottom of this, once and for all."

I waited for him to say more, but he opened his book again. Nobody else said anything, but it felt really funny in the room. I wanted to cry, to tell everyone I was sorry, but the words never came. Instead, I ate and dreamed about what it would be like to be able see what everyone else saw.

"Where do you think you're going?" Mom asked when I left the table.

I turned around, wondering why she sounded so angry. "Outside?"

"Do you think I'm so daft I can't see what you've

done? Now, get to your room. I'll deal with you later."

I remembered my jeans, and as I felt Mom's eyes burning into me, my legs shook beneath their wetness. *She's right*, I thought miserably, *I am the most horrible thing in the world.* I ran to our room, pulled off my jeans, and waited. Finally, the milk pails clanged together, and the back door slammed. Daddy was leaving to do the milking. I knew it was time and began to sob. I heard the swishing sound of the strap being yanked off the chimney, and Mom strode into the room with it dangling from her hand.

"Get up."

"I'm sorry," I begged, "I didn't do it on purpose, it just happened."

"Same old story." She grabbed my arm. "Just like this game with your eyes."

The first lash landed on my back, and I screamed for mercy.

"Shut up, if you know what's good for you."

She hit me repeatedly.

When I could scream no more, she released my arm and I fell to the floor. "Get into bed," she said, on her way out the door. "And if you tell your dad, you'll get twice as much."

The Glasses

I climbed into bed, and the rough flannelette sheets scraped against the welts. I pushed my hands between the sheets and the sorest stripes, but the sweat on my palms made the welts sting worse than the sheets did. I pulled my arms from beneath the covers and lay still, counting the throbs and praying to die.

It was dark, and Pat was fast asleep before the throbbing stopped. Even then, I couldn't sleep. All night long, I floated between wanting to die and wondering what it would be like to see what everyone else could see. Finally, the frogs on the slough behind the house started croaking, and Cocky Locky crowed in a new day. I pulled the covers tighter around my neck and waited for Daddy to start the fires.

Two o'clock that afternoon, Mom and I climbed the stairs to the second floor in the only hotel in town. At the end of a long, dark hallway, four chairs stood against the wall. Mom sat on the closest one to a closed door, and I climbed on the one beside it.

We waited and waited. At last, a white, skinny man

who smelled of cigarettes came out. "Are you Judith?"

I nodded, wiggling closer to Mom.

"Let's take a look."

We followed him inside the room. The room was empty except for a bed, two chairs, and a desk. Nothing that would fix broken eyes! I bit the back of my hand. The man sat at the desk and wrote. Then, spinning around on his chair, he reached for my face. I jerked back, hiding behind Mom's arm.

"Don't be so foolish." She pushed me forward again. "He's not going to hurt you."

I wiggled to the edge of my chair. *That's easy for her to say. She's not little, and her eyes aren't broken.*

"Can I look now?"

I nodded, grasping the sides of my chair until my fingers went numb.

He put a long shiny thing over one of my eyes. It lit up and started clicking. I saw his eye looking at mine. "Interesting," he mumbled over and over again. "I can give her glasses," he told Mom in a really slow way, as if he was still thinking. "But she needs a specialist."

"What?" Mom gasped. "You mean there *is* something wrong?"

"Very much."

The Glasses

He put the funniest looking glasses on my face and kept changing the glass in them. Gradually, the black blotches on his chart turned into letters. "I can see!" I shouted, clapping my hands. "I can see."

He took the glasses off my face and smiled. A warm, *I like you* smile.

Happiness hugged my insides, but only until I pictured myself at school wearing a smaller version of the contraption I'd just had on. The other kids were pointing and laughing.

"No!" I yelled. "Please don't make me wear them."

He rumpled my hair, laughing softly. "These are just a tool I use to make glasses. I'll mail you the prettiest ones I have."

One week later, they came. I tore the box open, put them on, and ran outside. Everything looked different. Grass and clover separated. The green dresses I thought trees wore became millions of little green leaves. Blue and purple mountains reached so high into the sky that I was sure God lived on them. I glanced up the tree beside me. For the first time in my life, I saw a little brown bird sitting on a branch, and I burst into tears.

Sleep played hide-and-seek with me that night. Time before sunrise stood still, or it felt like it did, but eventually sunbeams streamed into the bedroom window. I dressed in my best school clothes and wolfed down my breakfast. "Hurry up," I hollered at Pat. "We'll be late."

In front of the school, all the other kids were lined up in a Red Rover game. I ran to the centre of the game. "Look. I can see. I'm not blind anymore!"

No one said a word. They just stared. Finally, Susan broke out laughing. "Four eyes," she shouted. "That's what we can call her now. Four eyes."

I yanked my glasses off my face and ran sobbing to the school. "I hate you," I wanted to scream at the kids behind me, but I knew better. That would just make things worse.

Miss Hall met me at the door. "What's the matter?" she asked, taking my glasses from my hand. "They're very pretty. Can I see them on you?"

I put them on and looked at her.

"What do you see?" she asked.

"You!" I exclaimed, letting my excitement return. "You have a real face instead of a light-coloured ball."

Tears came into her eyes, and she bent down and

hugged me. "Needing glasses is nothing to be ashamed of. You might have to work a little harder than others, but you're a very smart little girl, and there is no doubt in my mind that you can grow up to be whatever you choose to be."

I swelled on the inside and pushed out of her hug, so I could see her face. "Do you really mean that?" I asked, unable to believe my ears. "I can be whatever I want, even if I can hardly see without my glasses?"

She nodded.

I looked at the Red Rover game. "Does that mean I'm good enough to play with the other kids?"

Her smile disappeared. "You are just as good as anyone else. Never forget it."

"Really?" I asked, already running across the schoolyard to the Red Rover game. "Look out, here I come."

TOUCHED BY AN ANGEL

by Rebecca Blaevoet

CW: Religious themes, fear of harm

Fifteen years ago, my mother celebrated a significant birthday. A surprise party had been planned for her, in a city several hours from where I worked.

I resolved to go, of course, but had to make the trip fit into my schedule.

Finishing work late on a Friday afternoon meant that I had to jump onto the train, bright and early on Saturday morning, leap off at the other end, pounce on the first taxi I could find, wrestle the "Yes-I'll-take-your-dog" commitment out of the driver, and dash to the party before the birthday girl arrived at 1:00 p.m. After a mere twelve hours with my family, I was obliged to book a ticket on the returning night bus, departing at 1:00 a.m. the next morning, and arrive on the doorstep of my church, barely coherent, a couple of hours prior to the start of the service. I was the choir director after all.

I had a small window to work with: Friday evening to Sunday morning. It was the sort of thing I loved doing—a bit over the top, slightly madcap, but a good lark, nonetheless. Truth be told, the tight itinerary was half the fun. A whirlwind 24-hour trip was as much part of the adventure as the main event: the surprise party. Besides, it was just starting to be full summer and the sunny, warm world felt optimistic, charged with energy and a whole lot of holiday.

Early summer where my mother lives is splendid, especially if you're a sun-worshipper like me. It's always mid-90s there by the first week of July, and the best thing on earth is a picnic on a patio, with music, a barbecue, and people in good humour. If it were possible to throw in a lake, for good measure, that would be even better, but you can't ask for everything in this life.

The party was perfect. The tablecloths flapped in the breeze, the barbecue wafted, the balloons bobbed on their strings, poinging abstractedly off your head if you inadvertently walked into one, as if to say: "Enjoy yourselves, everyone! We're here, too." Extended family, extended tables, extended warmth.

My mom has always been the undisputed life of the

party, and after she got over her tongue-tied, teary surprise (and was she surprised!), she came through with flying colours! Then she was the hostess, the MC, the comedy act, and the ringleader.

It was really quite a bash, one of those memories one has of being utterly embraced by a celebration. It's good to have those glittering, sparkling moments to look back upon, with affection, across the intervening years.

As the sun drifted toward the west and guests drifted toward their cars, my sister, mother, and I drifted toward the kitchen, glasses of wine in our hands, to finish the clean-up.

As sure as twilight was creeping into the backyard, a clammy sort of cold was beginning to settle on me, too. I started to picture the hours ahead. At this moment, I was enveloped by my family, still aglow with the light of the summer afternoon, but I would soon be among total strangers, out in the dark.

I never feel that a Saturday night is quite as safe a time to be out and about as other nights. I really prefer to be indoors, cozy in my own house, or in the company of friends with a sure way of getting to my own door and closing it behind me, by the time night falls. Maybe that comes from having been an urban dweller for a lot of my life and having had to rely on public transit for most of that time. One becomes attuned to where the sirens are, or if loud voices are raised in the street below, or worse.

So, despite my sinking heart, I took comfort from the fact that I wouldn't have to wait at the bus station long, and that the trip itself lasts at least five hours. I always make sure to take the seat on the bus across from the driver and engage him or her in conversation for a minute, right at the start of a journey, thus rendering myself less invisible. I do enjoy a long bus trip, profiting from the hours to read, study something interesting, knit, listen to music—in other words, catch up on things I never seem to have time to do during my regular life. On this occasion, however, I wished that the return logistics could have been different.

At midnight, I was calling yet another cab to take me to the bus station. The day had been wonderful, glowing, fleeting as a northern summer, but already I was regretting my choice of attire. My sundress had seemed so liberating and celebratory at 7:00 a.m. that morning. Now it seemed flimsy, revealing, provocative. I felt exposed, vulnerable, and completely unprepared for a Saturday night outside the closed bus station at the corner of two main streets in the red-light district.

No matter, I thought, the bus will be here soon.

At 12:55 a.m., an inspector strode by, announcing in a disinterested voice that the bus had been delayed across the river for at least an hour, and we'd be given more information when they knew anything. Now you see him, now you don't! He disappeared as quickly as he appeared, almost as if he didn't want to be caught up in whatever drama might be unfolding. Too much paperwork, no doubt!

There was some murmuring among the half-dozen people sitting on the benches with me, outside the closed bus station. And then I heard them all get up and walk away. *Oh no*, I thought, *this block is wall-to-wall bars… and now everybody has left. So much for safety in numbers.*

The bus station was located in a town square of sorts, surrounded by the main drag, the access route to the commuter tunnel, and the two side streets that would take you directly to the casino. It was also a block up from the street where all the action was, after everywhere else turned out the lights. In its starkest terms, the bus station was located on the *happeningest* parking lot on a Saturday night, and the place to be, if you had money to spend, liquor to drink, and especially if you were hunting game. The diviest bars, the wildest partiers, the biggest fights—sex for sale, booze for sale, and many, many people out to buy.

Even while wearing a business suit, carrying a briefcase, and walking briskly, a young woman might not feel particularly safe in that area during the day. A blind woman, rightly or wrongly, might be encouraged to keep away from there, unless accompanied by a sighted person. I know I had been, when I worked in that city, years before! And here I was, past midnight, in July, wearing less than a yard of some synthetic flowery window dressing, with a marshmallow of a Labrador guide dog at my feet, in a deserted parking lot, surrounded by buildings whose windows were not looking toward a concrete wasteland. I certainly did not feel safe.

On Saturday night, kids who were below the legal age in the next county would cross the river and flock to local bars. The streets around the bus station catered to that demographic, almost entirely. I had a cousin who worked at one of them and he told me that Saturday night, (well, really Sunday morning) between

1:00–3:00 a.m. was the busiest time in the entire week.

I felt an adrenaline rush of terror as I heard the sluice gates open, and the desolate inner city parking lot begin to fill with teeming crowds of people.

I began to feel like I was on display, a sitting duck, unprotected, planted as I was, stoically on my bench, dressed for a pool party, with my ridiculously expensive-looking braille notetaker in my hands, easily snatched, easily sold in the blink of an eye, with complete impunity. This was also before the days of the iPhone, remember, so there was no concept of texting my sister to let her know what was happening.

Heart rate picking up, I was on the verge of heading for the building with the most noise, in hopes that at a bare minimum, there might be a phone I could use to call someone, when someone sat down beside me.

"Yes, it's a nice night!" she said in a deep, slow voice.

My first impulse was to keep to my plan and walk away, afraid I would be in more trouble if it looked like I knew the person harassing me than if I was a lone traveller. I couldn't detect the smell of alcohol, or even tobacco smoke, so I deduced that I wouldn't be subjected to an hour of rambling, intoxicated jibber-jabber, but I didn't understand what she was doing there or why she should choose to take a seat right beside me, when there seemed to be acres of empty benches to my left and right. Now, I felt trapped.

"Bus late again?" she asked. "They always are, get held up on the other side of the bridge, I guess."

"Yes, that's what the inspector said." A bit short, a bit dismissive. Maybe I should try and make polite conversation till I know what's what. "Are you waiting for it?" *Let's discover a little about this person,* I thought.

"No, I'm just heading across the river. "

That seemed safe. At least she wouldn't stay long. She was probably just taking a breather, saw me sitting here by myself, and thought she'd be friendly. *What a kind thing to do,* I reflected, as I settled back down onto the cold, wooden bench.

"You looked like you could use some company."

I certainly could!

She asked me about my trip, the day, my work, my choir, all in the same, peaceful, slow manner of speaking. We talked about the recent cross-county festivities, the summer fireworks, and many other things. The time passed imperceptibly, and I slowly felt my tension melting away. I was sure that it was her steady voice and easy conversation that were soothing my jangled nerves and putting me at ease.

Waves of people drifted across our parking lot—closing time here, still another hour there, main drag, commuter tunnel access, casino to and fro, bars, bars, and more bars. Tourists from both sides of the river passed us in their thousands and still no bus. But the atmosphere that had seemed so ominous and threatening now seemed friendly, a bit raucous, but harmless. I wondered if the bus would come at all, but I was happy to have a companion while I waited. In fact, I was extremely relieved.

At about 3:30 a.m. she eased herself to her feet and said, "Well I best be getting on my way. I expect your bus will be here soon."

"I've really enjoyed our talk," I responded. "Thank you for keeping me company. I wasn't feeling very safe here, I must say."

"You'll be alright now. God bless you, honey."

"You too. Are you really crossing the river?"

"That's what I'm going to do, go across the river." She sauntered away, humming comfortably to herself.

I marvelled at how the last two hours had flown by. Then I started worrying again. Surely, I hadn't missed the bus, had I? It was supposed to pull up right in front of me, wasn't it? What if it went to a different door while we had been talking? She would have seen it. I would have heard it... surely. I could feel anxiety tightening its grip under my rib cage and again was on the verge of getting up, planning to go in search of someone, when the inspector walked through once more, announcing that the bus would be here in five minutes and that we should have our tickets ready. Big sigh, grateful, rather apologetic prayer of thanks.

A crowd was gathering little by little, so I took my place with the rest in line, fishing for my tickets in my purse.

Sure enough, the bus rolled up in a matter of moments, and we all stumbled on board, half asleep and cold.

Gratefully, I sank into a seat and calculated that I wouldn't be so early for church after all. I put my head back and closed my eyes. It had been a remarkable day, brimming with sensations and extremes. Exhaustion sent me tumbling into oblivion, before I'd even had a chance to speak to the driver! I have no recollection of the next day, but presumably I made it to church and directed the choir.

Years later, now married, my husband and I had the wonderful opportunity of moving back to my hometown. Much remained the same, but several significant changes had taken place. They had relocated the bus terminal, for one, pulling it out of its art deco building in the heart of downtown, and constructing a new, modern thing a few blocks west, with traffic islands and bus lanes—the bane of every blind person. Most of the dive bars were gone, along with a good deal of the business on the main drag. For some inexplicable reason, I found that rather sad.

There was a lot of talk about the new bridge being built. It would have bike lanes and maybe even a pedestrian walkway so people without a car could cross to the other side.

I asked a city councillor about it, my mind flashing vividly on the night, years previous, when I had been tossed and turned on that strange sea of revelry, and the kind woman who had stopped to keep me company.

"How do pedestrians get across the river now?" I enquired.

His answer was simple, succinct, and stopped me in my tracks:

"You can't," was all he said.

THE BLOOD TREES

by Jamieson Wolf

CW: Grief accompanying a new diagnosis, depression

The forest came for him at night.

It hadn't always been this way. He tried to picture the world as it had been before, and the world after, and wondered if there had always been a third world. He thought that there had to be. Time didn't matter much to him anymore; now there was only light, darkness, and the uncertainty of time forgotten.

When Jackson was diagnosed, he'd become lost within himself. The deep rivers of sadness that ran underneath his skin had unnerved him at first, but eventually, he welcomed the coolness of their waters. He looked forward to losing time and himself within their dark, wet terrain. One evening, as he was following the path of the river within him, he came upon the forest.

Its trees pulsed with shadows, the leaves a green so dark that it resembled pitch blackness. He went back to the forest each night, venturing a little further with each visit. It was the whisper of the leaves that called to him.

Often, he got lost and couldn't find the spot where he had entered the forest. The trees would close around him and did not want to let him go.

In the morning, he would lie in bed and think on what he had discovered. He wondered if he went too far into the forest, would he be able to wake again? He didn't want to find out, and yet, it was another case of *before-and-after*. Before, he would not have spent all day in bed. Now, during his waking hours, he yearned for sleep and the solace the dark forest provided.

His diagnosis should not have come as a shock. His brother had been diagnosed with multiple sclerosis a year earlier, and they were twins. Chances had been good that Jackson had multiple sclerosis, too. Jackson hadn't wanted to believe them, and he had put off getting tested for as long as possible. However, when he had lost the ability to type, had difficulty speaking, and had gone blind, he decided to go ahead with the testing.

Jackson didn't mind not being able to speak. It was the blindness and the loss of the ability to type that bothered him most. It felt like two different kinds of blindness at once. He had known the keyboard so well, and now it was unfamiliar territory. His brain had forgotten the paths to find the right keys. Jackson kept telling himself that he hadn't lost all his sight. He could get around with help and by relying on the kindness of others. He could discern different places and objects, but whenever he looked at people, he noticed his blindness the most. The details of people's faces, like their eyes and facial features, had been wiped clean.

The doctors had told him that the blindness was only temporary, that it would likely improve. It would take time, they said. It had been several months now, and while most of his sight had returned, the temporary blindness struck at odd moments. Usually at night, if there was low lighting or if he fought fatigue. It had become, like all his other symptoms, an unwelcome house guest. The only escape was within the forest, but after months of travelling its pathways, he didn't feel sure he belonged there anymore either. Still, he could not stay away. Jackson went to the forest every night, hoping for respite, wanting to lose himself perhaps forever among the blackened leaves. The forest had begun to fill his mind so completely, he wasn't surprised to find leaves creeping along the walls of his apartment, even during the daylight hours.

One evening, when he'd become particularly lost in

the forest, venturing further than he ever had before, he'd tripped and grabbed at some nearby branches to stop his fall. Jackson had felt a hot slash of pain on the palm of his hand, and was startled to find a line of blood there. The tree had taken its price. He'd wondered how much flesh it would demand from him.

After the bloodletting, the shadows of trees became more pronounced. It got so that he could hear the whisper of the trees during the day, and the sporadic caws of birds would wake him from his slumber. The forest had become so much a part of his sleeping and his waking, Jackson wondered if he would ever be able to separate himself from it again.

Which was why he was so surprised to discover someone else in his forest. He had begun to see footsteps that didn't belong to him, and could smell new scents over the smell of damp earth—a hint of spice and something that reminded him of sandalwood. As much as he wanted to stay away from whoever was in the forest, Jackson couldn't help but be drawn to the stranger.

He had never discovered anyone else in the forest in all the months that he had been visiting it. This was his forest and his alone, or so he thought. Tonight, when he had entered the forest, Jackson tried to get a good look at the intruder, following his footsteps on the leaves. Jackson could make out his shape moving amongst the trees. He blinked several times, hoping that his vision would clear. It remained stubbornly blurry.

"For fuck sakes," he whispered.

Jackson moved closer. He could tell the man stood by the river that ran through the forest. He could hear it nearby. Jackson knew that the man was tall and broad-shouldered, but that was all he could tell from this distance. Hiding behind a tree, Jackson wondered what he should do. He had no idea who the man was or even if it was safe to approach him. This unknown man could be violent or mean him harm—Jackson had no way of knowing. While he was trying to decide whether or not to move out from behind the tree where he hid, a dark crow cawed overhead, and the man turned and looked right at him; at least, Jackson thought the man was looking at him. The man's head turned in Jackson's direction, at any rate.

Jackson stayed where he was, hoping that he remained invisible to this stranger behind one of the blood trees. He tried to stay as still as he could, hoping that the man would leave and go far away from here. However, the man just stayed where he was. Jackson heard him let out a sigh.

"I know you're there," the man said. "I can see you."

Jackson wondered if this was a trick, if his vision made him see things more than usual. He often tried to fill in the blind spots with random bits of flotsam and jetsam, his mind adding details like an eye, an ear, or the curve of a mouth. The pieces never fit properly, but he'd felt this was better than looking at the blankness of nothing.

"I'm not going to hurt you," the man said, his voice soft with a rasp in it.

"That's a likely story," Jackson said softly, though his own voice amplified much more than its regular volume. The forest did this; it warped the sounds that were made within its trees. It was why the crows cawed louder. It was also probably why his heartbeat pounded so loudly in his ears.

"Fine," the man said. "I'll come to you then."

Jackson was filled with fear now. He'd assumed that the man might be a figment of his imagination, but as the man walked towards him, each step making noise as the man stepped on the grass and twigs of the forest floor, Jackson had to admit this was not likely. He had never known a figment of his imagination to make noise before.

With the final crack of a twig, the man stood in front of Jackson. He tried blinking, but the light around the man's head wouldn't clear, and Jackson couldn't discern the details of the man's face.

He held out his hand, and Jackson stared at it for a moment before taking it. It looked to be a normal hand, though Jackson would not put it past the forest to send a goblin or some other monster to take more flesh from him. The forest had had its drop of flesh; what was to say that it didn't want more?

"I won't bite, unless you ask me to," said the man.

Jackson's blood raced momentarily at those words. He gave a sharp nod and took the man's hand. It was strong and warm and what was more, he could see the man's facial features and the forest around him looked brighter. He had striking blue eyes and a messy mop of black hair with stubble along his chin.

"I'm Jackson."

"It's nice to meet you. I'm Clive."

They held hands for a moment longer and then parted. When they did so, Jackson's eyesight faded once again. He let out a sigh when what he wanted to do was hold on to Clive for as long as possible. What magic made him see his face so clearly? Was it a trick of the blood trees? Would the forest take this from him too after giving it to him so briefly? He shook his head and heard Clive chuckle.

"Is something funny?" Jackson asked.

"You just seem to be having quite the conversation with yourself inside your head. Come on, let's get you out from behind the trees. Let's go take a walk."

"I still don't know what you're doing in my forest."

"I've always thought of this place as *my* forest. I've never seen *you* here before." He held out his hand again. "Come on, let's go take a walk. Have you seen the mica mine?"

Jackson shook his head. "No, I try to get myself lost in the trees a lot. I keep thinking that this time, I won't be able to find my way out again."

"That's pretty deep. Are you always so morose?" Clive reached out and took Jackson's hand.

When Jackson looked at Clive again, he could see his features, could see how the moonlight in the forest was shining in his blue eyes and made them look as if they were silver. It felt odd to be holding the hand of a person he had just met, but Jackson was so happy to see clearly that he didn't pull his hand away.

He let Clive pull him out from behind the blood trees. Jackson could even see the trees of the forest more clearly. Before, he was able to see the branches of the trees, the leaves that waved in the wind, and the pathways that he walked. Now, he could see the blackened wood of the trees, how the feathers of the birds within the trees shone like tar, and could even see the occasional spiderweb that hung from some of the branches. Clive took him to the water, and Jackson noticed the water was almost black. They stood there for a moment, and Jackson breathed in the damp smell of the water and the mulch that had begun to remind him of home. This worried him.

"You're doing it again," Clive said.

"What am I doing?"

"You're thinking so loud, I'm surprised the trees themselves aren't shaking."

"Can you hear what I'm thinking?" Jackson asked.

"I didn't say that. I can see it in your face. There is a storm going on behind your eyes, and it looks tumultuous."

Jackson let out a snort. "And you'd know all about

storms, of course."

"Yes," Clive said. "I would. I wouldn't be here if I didn't carry my own." His voice had taken on a harsh tone.

This gave Jackson pause. He wondered at what Clive had been through for him to end up here. "Why are you in my forest?" he asked.

"As I've said before, I've always thought of this as *my* forest. I've walked these pathways for what feels like years. Too long, really. Far too long." He shook his head. "I'm so sick of these trees and what they have taken from me."

"And what did they take from you?"

"Everything." There was pain in this word. "Everything." Clive repeated.

They began to walk away from the water. Though there was no wind, the leaves around them moved so it sounded like the forest was whispering around them, and maybe it was. That made him think of another question.

"I thought that the forest was within me," Jackson said. "That it was mine to wander alone."

"I thought that too at first," Clive said.

They had come upon a rock wall that Jackson had

never seen before. It was covered in dark water that slid down from above, making it seem as if the rocks were made of glass. Jackson saw shapes moving within the water and wondered what else he would find if he stared long enough. Clive led him a little further beyond it, and there was an opening made from the rocks. It looked like a doorway, and Jackson could see light sparkling from within.

"I've discovered quite a few people here," said Clive. "I never approached them though; they were going their own way. They would appear like shadows given shape as they walked along their own paths." He pulled Jackson gently into the rock opening. "Over time, I came to realize that the forest is within all of us. It's a portal, really."

"What do you mean by that?" Jackson asked. He felt like laughing but didn't. The rocks around them that sparkled with light seemed to demand reverence.

"Well, we all carry a river of sadness within. A river of emotions that run deep. Sometimes, we get lost among it and follow it for longer than is good for us. Some people never leave the forest, the call of the trees can be so strong. Other times, people get lost and can never find their way back out again."

The Blood Trees

Jackson wanted to ask Clive how he knew so much about the forest. Jackson had had the very same thoughts about the leaves and water that whispered to him like a lover. He thought of asking Clive about what the trees had taken from him but realized quickly that it didn't matter. They were all walking their own path, like the shadow people that Clive had seen.

Clive gently pulled Jackson a little deeper into the cavern. The walls sparkled brightly, the light seeming to come from within the walls themselves. Clive let go of Jackson's hand and reached out and broke off a piece of the wall. When Clive placed the piece of the wall into Jackson's hand, Clive's fingers touched Jackson's palm and his vision was clear again, only for a second.

"This is mica," Clive said. "It's a mineral that is formed in layers. Those layers reflect the light in different ways, kind of like a multifaceted mirror. See?" He moved the piece in Jackson's palm and Jackson watched as the light changed and moved. It made the mica look as if it were alive.

"It's beautiful," Jackson said.

"We're all kind of like this piece of mica."

"How so?"

"We're all formed by layers—one moment at a time

shaping us and our journey, you know? That even amongst all the darkness we carry with us, we always find ways to shine."

Clive closed Jackson's hand over the piece of mica, and left his hand there. Jackson wondered if the light of the stone had grown brighter in the darkness. Jackson could certainly feel it, and the light pulsed within him. Jackson looked up at Clive, into his blue eyes, and could see the storm that they contained was still, just for this moment. Jackson hardly dared to breathe. When Clive moved towards him, Jackson didn't even think about pulling away from him There was a spark that ran through the air and Jackson breathed it in, tasted the lightning on his tongue. When their lips finally touched, Jackson had to close his eyes, because the small cavern had erupted in light.

He could feel the light. It was nothing compared to the heat he felt from Clive's lips, which spread throughout him. He was reminded of something that his mother said to him once when he was younger. *"We see more clearly with our hearts than we do with our eyes, Jacky boy. It's when we see from our hearts that we finally know where we are going."* He hadn't known what she had meant until now.

When the kiss ended, Jackson found himself already wishing for more. Gazing at Clive, Jackson realized that this was the first time he had felt alive in ages.

"Thank you."

"Thank *you*, Jackson," Clive said. "You made my last venture into this forest a worthwhile one."

Panic swept through Jackson. "Your last visit? Why won't you be coming back?"

Clive took Jackson's hand again and led him out of the mica mine, back towards the river. "I've had enough of this." He motioned at the forest, at the blood trees.

When Jackson looked at them, the leaves had tips of red. It was as if they were crying out the blood that they had already taken.

"I want more for my life than to lose myself so completely here," Clive said. "Don't you?"

Jackson nodded, surprising himself. He hadn't known until then that he wanted to leave the forest, too.

"Yes, I do, but I'm afraid to leave. It's all I've known for so long."

"Life has so much more to offer you, Jackson. Don't you want to experience it instead of being frightened of what it can give you?"

Nodding once more, Jackson knew that he no longer wanted to be afraid. "If we never come here again, how will I be able to find you?"

Clive kissed him softly, the light around them brightening once more. "Sometimes, the heart has a way of making things work. We know each other on a deeper level than most people now. Love will find a way."

Jackson stared at Clive's face and wondered if it would be the last time that he would be seeing him. "I've never been in love."

"Well, then maybe it's time for a change. Goodbye for now, Jackson. I'll be seeing you soon."

Jackson was the one to kiss Clive this time, and he leaned forward as if propelled to do so. When they broke apart, Clive gave him a smile and walked away into the blood trees. Jackson watched him go until he could no longer make out his shape in the trees. He watched for a moment longer, wondering if Clive would return. After a few minutes, Jackson knew that he was truly alone in the forest. He began to walk along the path of the water as he had when he had first come upon the forest. It had been so long since he had done this. For months now, he had simply fallen asleep, surrounded by the shadows of the trees on his walls, and found himself there. He had never purposely sought to find his way home.

As he walked, he felt a shift within him. He reached out and grabbed hold of a leaf from one of the blood trees at the edge of the forest. While he knew that he could not remain here, he also could not forget everything that the forest had taught him. Tucking the leaf into his back pocket, he walked onward, leaving the forest and the small river behind him. He had never walked so far away from his sadness before.

His apartment was there to welcome him, the same as it always had been. While the shadows of the trees remained upon his walls, they were different; they seemed to be softer. He looked around him and while not everything was clear, Jackson felt that he was *seeing* for the first time in months. Jackson could still hear the wind and the leaves still moved, but the shadows seemed paler and more translucent, the sounds of the forest muted. It would be a long time until the shadows left, if at all, but he knew that every step he took now was one that went along a new path from the one that he had been walking.

Looking at himself in the mirror, Jackson leaned in close. He didn't appear to be any different, but he knew the changes were on the inside, and that was what mattered.

There was a knock on his apartment door. Jackson took one moment to make sure that he looked somewhat presentable and went to answer it. He had a feeling he knew who would be on the other side of the door.

Jackson smiled. Tonight, he would choose a different path than the one he had been walking on.

NOA AND THE DRAGON

by Jameyanne Fuller

CW: Ableism and internalized ableism

When the fever passed, Noa woke to darkness. Someone breathed to her right. Someone else sobbed. "Daddy?" Her voice was hoarse.

"How do you feel, Noa?" Her father touched her forehead. It was too dark to see him.

"Daddy, is it nighttime?"

"No, Noa darling. It's afternoon."

That made sense. She could hear the clip-clop of horses and the rumble of carts down in the street. A herald shouted about the cure for the white fever, and a ghost speaker swore she could reach loved ones lost to the illness. Water rushed in the aqueduct overhead, and a vendor pushed a cart of sizzling hot fool's gold triangles past their house—she could smell the spicy dough pockets and hear the clack of the cart's wheels on the street tiles.

Noa blinked, but the world remained dark. "Daddy,

I can't see. Everything's dark." Her voice rose. "It's all dark, Daddy!"

"I know, Noa." Her father took her hand. His fingers were rough and dry. "The healers came. They brought down your fever. You're going to be fine. But—but they said it was too late to—even with their magic they couldn't—Noa, baby, you're blind."

Shivers racked her that had nothing to do with the fever. "Everything's black," she whispered.

Beside her father, her mother sobbed. She lifted Noa half out of bed into her arms, cradling Noa's face against her shoulder.

"You're going to be fine." Her father squeezed her hand. He put his other hand on the back of her head. "I've already talked to the Fijen Temple."

"Kyan, not now." Her mother lowered Noa back into bed and stroked her hair. "Isn't it bad enough?"

"I thought the Fijen Temple just protected people," Noa said.

"They help people," her father said, "and they've been researching how to help people like you for years. It will take them a few weeks to pull everything together for you—there are a lot of people who were sick and lost their sight or hearing—but they've promised to do it as quickly as possible. We won't let this stop you, Noa. You'll be just like everybody else."

"But it's all black." Her eyes were wide open. She knew there was a blue ceiling above her, crossed with birch beams that would be tangled with afternoon sunlight, but all she could see was darkness. Absolute darkness. And her mother kept sobbing.

Noa's world narrowed to her bed.

There was her pillow, her blankets, the foot of the mattress on either side of her, her raggedy doll. She could feel this, but beyond the bed was unknown.

She could never be like everyone else again, whatever her father said. She could not see.

At night, her parents argued.

"She needs to get out of bed," her father said.

Noa could not hear her mother's response.

"It's not nonsense," her father said furiously. "Fijen—"

"Fijen doesn't care about us or Noa. What they told you—it's just to stop you from feeling sorry for yourself.

If Fijen really cared, Noa wouldn't be blind."

Silence stretched through the house. Noa felt it press against her face as if it were alive. At last, her father said, "Noa just needs to learn she can do it."

"Have you ever tried to walk around with your eyes closed, Kyan?"

"She *can* do it."

After that, her father insisted Noa get up and start learning her way around the house again. She knew their tall, skinny house, of course, one of many crammed together under the aqueduct at the edge of Seaview. But now it was full of dangers: shelves and cupboards to crack her head on; narrow doorways to knock her shoulders; steep, uneven stairs to catch her feet and send her sprawling.

Still, her father insisted.

Five steps to her bedroom door. Her father made her count. Five steps, then the soft rug changed to wood that gave and creaked under her feet. Turn right. Three paces to the stairs. Then down fifteen stairs. The stairs were slightly crooked, their edges softened from wear— she hadn't noticed before—but she had the banister to guide her. Turn left into the kitchen. The heat from the hearth pressed the right side of her face.

Her father made her sit at the table. He put a plate in front of her—fragrant steam rose to her nose—and said she would feed herself. They started small—couscous, chickpeas, and leeks, which she could roll into balls with her fingers and dunk into a spicy ginger sauce. Then garlic noodles which her father cut so she could use a spoon. But then things got more complicated.

"Your plate is a circle," he said. "The chicken is at the top of the plate, farthest away from you. The turnips are on the left. The spinach is on the right. Do you understand?"

"Daddy, it's too hard."

"The plate is in front of you. Find it with your left hand."

Slowly, tentatively, Noa reached out her left hand. Her fingers brushed the table, then the curved edge of the plate.

"Now use your fork to find the food," her father said. "It's already cut up."

"Kyan—"

"She can do this, Fiella. Come on, Noa. Take a bite."

Noa felt around with the fork, found a piece of something, and stabbed it. The tines of the fork screeched across the plate. "Daddy—"

"Try again."

If her father was at work, her mother did not make her get out of bed or feed herself. She held Noa's hand and sang until her voice was hoarse. She said Noa's father loved Noa very much, but he couldn't accept what had happened. Once he did, he would stop making Noa do things that were too hard for her.

Then her father brought the books. He sat by her bed late into the night and read to her. She closed her eyes so she could ignore the darkness and let the words fill her up. She could picture it all. She could live it all.

First were the people who were banished because they believed the world was round when everyone still thought it was a cube. They disappeared over the mountains at the top of the world, and no one ever found out what happened to them.

Next was the boy who raised an injured dragon until they were able to defend his village together.

There were ships on rolling seas, daring sword fights

on cliffs, magicians who spoke to the gods. She imagined mountains disappearing into the skies, dense green forests, rolling hills and farmland stretching to the sea, cities sparkling like jewels.

"I wish I could really see it," she said one night as her father closed the book and pulled her blankets up to her chin.

"But you can see it, Noa, if you want to."

"No, I can't." How could he say she could see anything?

"Just because you can't see it doesn't mean it isn't there for you to explore." He kissed her cheek and left the room.

The next night, her father was late. Noa sat up, waiting for the next story he would bring her. It was the first time she'd been excited for anything since the fever.

But when he finally returned, he did not sit by the bed. "I have a surprise for you, Noa."

Noa slid out of bed and found her shoes, tucked under the nightstand where she'd left them. She tied her shoes, then looked up at her father. "I did it myself." It was the first time.

"Do you want to see what else you can do?" He took

her hand and wrapped it around a stick. It was polished wood. There was a cold metal cap on the bottom, and the top was carved to fit her hand. Standing up, it was as tall as her collarbone. But it wasn't meant to stand vertically. It was a guiding staff, and she was meant to sweep it in front of her to find her way herself.

Noa moved around her bedroom, tapping the guiding staff in front of her like her father showed her. She found the bed, the wardrobe, the desk where she'd done her schoolwork before the fever, then the doorway.

"What do you think?"

"I'm not sure." It felt clumsy in her hand. But she was standing in the middle of her room, and she knew where she was, not because she remembered what it looked like, but because she could feel all around her. Maybe she would feel better once she practiced.

"Come downstairs," her father said. "I have one more surprise."

He sat her at the table and placed something in front of her. From the way it landed, it sounded big. Noa propped her guiding staff against the table beside her, then reached out and explored it with her hands. It was bigger than a dinner plate and square, with a hard leather cover. When she opened it, she discovered heavy pages.

"It's a book," she cried, understanding. "But—" But the pages weren't smooth. They were covered in sharp points.

"It's for you," her father said. "This is how blind people read. I got it from the Fijen Temple. This is a novel, and I have another book to teach you how to read it."

"I didn't know I could," she whispered.

"Do you want to learn?"

"Yes. Yes, can we start now?"

"Here. We'll start with this." He took the book in front of her and replaced it with another, smaller one. She opened the book and ran her hands over the dots. They were sharp and insistent beneath her fingers. She wanted to understand what they meant. The chair beside her squeaked across the floor, and then her father took her wrist and guided her right hand to the top of the page.

"These dots are bigger," he said, "so you can learn. And these aren't the letters of the alphabet like you learned in school. Each combination of dots is a sound."

"Why?" Noa asked.

"Well, most people who are blind are born that way, and they never learn how to spell. So they made this language usable for everyone."

"Oh." Noa was disappointed. She'd learned the alphabet at school. Why couldn't she learn to spell like everyone else? And would she really be learning a different language?

"So," her father said, "just one dot, like this, is the sound 'ah.'"

From "ah," they went to "uh"—two dots aligned horizontally—and then to "ay"—three dots. The dots she'd first felt had been tiny, sharp, and confusing, but on the first page of this book, they were as large as the pad of her thumb. She insisted they go through all the sounds before they stopped.

Later, in bed with her fingers still skimming her new alphabet, Noa heard her parents arguing again.

"You're not doing her any good," her mother shouted. "You'll just hurt her, Kyan."

"That's not true. I'm giving her the tools to live in this world."

"You're giving her false hope. Unless she has a gift—"

"Noa doesn't need magic." Her father's voice rose

too. "All she needs is herself."

"Kyan." Her mother's voice dropped and took on the same soft, coaxing tone she'd used to explain multiplication to Noa before the fever. It was full of sadness, too. "All she'll ever be is a beggar. I pity her."

"Don't say that. Don't *ever* say that. Noa can do whatever she wants. She'll never be a beggar."

"Then I pity you too."

"Then leave." His voice was cold. "If you're not going to support this, if you're not going to support our daughter—"

"Kyan, don't—"

"I love you, Fia, but you're the one who's hurting her. If you're not going to help, you need to go."

"I love you, too, and I love Noa. But you're wrong about this." The front door opened, then closed behind her mother.

Noa's hands remained frozen on the symbol for "ch."

When at last the stairs creaked under her father's footsteps, Noa said, "Daddy?" He came in. "Is Mommy gone?"

"Yes." He sat beside her. "I'm sorry you heard that, Noa. I thought you were asleep. But you have to know, your mother loves you. She just doesn't understand. A lot of people aren't going to understand. But they'll see. They'll all see."

When her father left, Noa sat up and found the candle on her bedside table. She didn't know how to light it herself, but she wrapped her hands around the smooth, braided wax. "Fijen," she whispered. But what did she want to say? "Why is all this happening to us? What am I supposed to do? Daddy said I'm closer to you because I can't see, but—now Mommy's gone, and—" *And I feel so alone.*

In the dream, Noa sat cross-legged on the floor against a pile of cushions. Her fingers stroked satin. Heat touched her skin, and she breathed the warm, sharp smell of fire. Wood popped, and flames crackled and rushed.

"Drink, child," Fijen said. Her voice boomed in Noa's mind, yet it was as tender as her mother's had been before the fight.

"My mother said—"

"I do care. Of course I care. You have never been

alone." Fijen's skirts whispered like the hiss of the flames as she knelt before Noa. She pressed a rough wooden goblet into Noa's hands. It was warm, and Noa knew without needing to be told that it was full to the brim with fire. Noa brought the cup to her lips. The fire was hot, but it did not burn her. It tasted of chestnuts on winter nights, her favourite cinnamon tea, and butterscotch. Warmth filled her belly.

"You are strong, my child. But you must find the strength on your own. Find the courage inside you, and you will see. I will guide you as I can."

The goddess bent and kissed her forehead. A shock went through her, and Noa woke with a gasp. She could still taste chestnuts and cinnamon and butterscotch.

In the morning, Noa dressed herself, then found her guiding staff and her alphabet book. Five steps to the bedroom door. Turn right. Three steps to the stairs.

She stumbled on the top step but caught herself. *Find the courage inside you,* she told herself, but how could she do that, when her own mother didn't believe in her? And what did the goddess mean, "You will see?" The healers had said there was nothing to be done.

The warm, wheat-y scent of porridge met her nose as she turned into the kitchen.

"Daddy?"

"Look at you." His arms caught her up and spun her around. Noa dropped her guiding staff but clung to her alphabet book. Her staff rolled across the floor. Her father set her on her feet and a moment later placed her guiding staff back in her hand. Then he laughed. "I think we need a way for you to tell what colour your clothes are."

"Oh. What colours am I wearing?" She remembered colours. She missed them.

"Well, your skirt is purple, your blouse is orange, and your sweater is blue."

"Guess I don't match very well." Noa giggled. She must look ridiculous.

"I'll help you. Then how would you like to come to work with me?"

So that day, and every day after, Noa went with her father to the Seaview street guard station. While he walked his rounds, she sat on the floor in the corporal's office and read her alphabet book. The first pages showed the sounds in big dots, but the next pages showed them in smaller and smaller dots, until she was reading letters the size of the ones in the novel on her nightstand. The last pages of the book had whole words and sentences. Letter by letter, word by word, sentence by sentence, Noa taught herself to read.

She listened to the people in the street guard station as well—they always seemed to think she couldn't hear them. They talked about her father. They said he was a good street guard, and that he should be promoted soon. They said awful things about her mother. She was a street guard too, and they'd thought she was strong. But something had broken inside her. She should have been grateful Noa survived the fever at all. She shouldn't have abandoned them. Noa felt a hard knot clench in her stomach when she heard these things. A small voice in the back of her mind whispered that they were right, but Noa missed her mother too much to listen to it.

They talked about Noa too. Some of them, like her mother, thought her father was being ridiculous. But some said they were certain she would do whatever she set her mind to. Noa wished she felt that way herself. She was no longer afraid to leave her bed or disoriented and horrified by the blackness filling her open eyes. But the only time she felt powerful was when her hands flew across a page, her fingers tracing dots into words.

At night, when he thought she was asleep, her father cried. Noa slipped out of bed and found the novel she had not yet tried to read on her nightstand. She felt her way out of her room and around the corner to her father's room. She found the bed and crawled in beside him. And she began to read aloud.

"*Cas-Cassian and the Dragon*," she said. "Many years ago, when legends still walked the land, there lived a boy named Cassian." At first, her words were halting. But then, she became faster, more confident. "Cassian lived in a small village in the middle of a forest. When he was a child, he learned to hunt and pro- protect his village with his father and his brothers."

Her father sobbed harder.

"Daddy?"

"I didn't think she'd really leave," he said. "When I said that, I thought—"

Noa didn't know what to say. She couldn't blame her father. He had stayed. He had given her books. But he had told her mother to leave, and she missed her so much her heart ached.

But her mother could have stayed.

"Keep reading, Noa."

So Noa read on.

Cassian grew up. He became the strongest boy in the village. And then his favourite hunting falcon was wounded by a wild dog, and when Cassian lifted the injured bird, he slashed Cassian's face, destroying Cassian's right eye. Infection set in and spread to his left eye. Cassian went blind.

Her father stopped crying.

And Noa fell asleep, her head against his chest, her fingers still splayed on the open book. And in her dreams, she read on, her fingers gliding over the words like the skaters on the frozen canals at mid-winter.

Noa learned the route from home to the street guard station, and now when they walked, she did not hold her father's hand. She learned to pour milk without spilling and braid her hair by touch. Her father sewed differently shaped buttons into the seams of her clothes so she could match them herself.

He did not cry at night again, but Noa continued to read to him.

Cassian mourned his lost vision—his lost future.

Noa's father hung bells on all the doors so she could hear when they were opened. He nailed thin strips of wood to the floor in every doorway so she could tell when she was entering a room. Together, they reorganized the whole house so she could find everything herself.

Cassian learned of the dragons in the mountains with the power to restore his sight. His father carved two staves Cassian could use to guide him. He held them vertically, one in each hand, and planted them in the ground before him when he walked.

Noa learned the way to the bakery on the corner. Then to the butcher's up the hill. And finally, all the way to the Daymarket, where she stood, bewildered and scared, until she sorted through all the smells and sounds. The fountain gurgled ahead. To the left, someone shouted about fresh mangoes, and someone else claimed their blankets were the warmest in the whole city.

"And where are you now?" her father asked once she told him all this.

She inhaled. "There's bread. And cinnamon. And leather? And someone's hammering."

"Good," he said. "Directly on your left is a shoemaker. Next to that is a carpenter. And on your right is a baker. And up ahead, on the right, I see fried apples. If you can find them, we can buy a treat."

And Noa read. Pages and pages turned beneath her hands.

Cassian mastered the guiding staves and set off on his own to find the dragons.

One morning nearly four months after the fever, Noa woke to an empty house. Her father must have gone to work on the divorce papers with her mother again. Noa shouldn't have known about it, but she'd heard the street guards talking again—as if, because she was blind, she couldn't hear them.

So she dressed and brought her book downstairs. She would read with her father that night, but she was almost to the end, and she wanted to find out what happened. In the kitchen, she found the breakfast her father had left her by placing her book on top of it—two slices of bread and an apple. She brushed crumbs from the back cover of her book and ate.

She was just throwing the apple core into the bin under the wash basin when she heard the children shouting and laughing in the street and the clatter of a wooden ball on tile. Her friends. She hadn't seen them since before the fever—she'd been so focused on learning how to be blind—but now they were just outside, and she wasn't practicing with her father. She could show them her books and her guiding staff. Maybe she could play too. She grabbed her book and her guiding staff and went outside.

When she stepped down into the street, the laughter and shouting died. The ball clacked against the street tiles and rumbled to a stop.

"Noa?" a girl said. Noa thought it was her best friend, Arwen. Arwen's voice was uncertain. "What are you doing? Should you be out here all alone?"

"I heard you playing," Noa said. Now she felt uncertain herself. She'd thought they would be happy to see her. "Can I play too?"

To her left, a horse jingled and clip-clopped across the street on its way towards the market. Something scraped in front of her—a shoe scuffed against tile. They were looking at each other, Noa realized, talking without words, so she wouldn't know what they were thinking. She turned her head from side to side, trying to pick up even a whisper.

"I don't know, Noa," Arwen said at last.

"You can't do it," a boy said—was that Tash?—Noa wasn't sure. "It's too fast."

"No, I can. I can hear the ball and—" But she stopped. Her father said people wouldn't understand, but she'd never thought her own friends would close her out. She tightened her grip on her guiding staff. She shouldn't be surprised. Not after her mother left.

"Where's your father?" Arwen asked.

"He had to go out." Noa's voice was brittle. Any moment, it would crack, and she would start to cry. "He'll be back soon, I think."

"He's coming now," Tash said. "He's right up the street. Why don't you go meet him?"

"Tash, that's not—" Arwen started.

"No," Noa said. "I can do it. He's this way?" She gestured to her left, up the hill. If she showed them that she could walk up the street by herself to meet her father, then maybe they would let her play with them again.

"Yes," Tash said. "That way."

"Noa—"

But Noa turned, tucked her novel under her arm, and marched up the street.

There was a scuffle behind her, and Tash said, "Quit it, Arwen. Let her do it."

Noa kept to the left of the road, making sure every time she tapped her guiding staff to the left it touched grass and not tile. When the grass turned sharply to the left and the smell of fresh bread steamed out into the chilly air, she knew she had reached the bakery on the corner. If she took a right and crossed the street, she would be heading up towards the street guard station. She hesitated. Why hadn't her father called out to her?

"Keep going," Tash yelled.

She listened. She heard no carts or footsteps, so she crossed the street and continued up the hill. When the street curved to the right, she knew she had passed the road that dead-ended into their street and led up towards the market.

If they could see her father, shouldn't Noa have met him by now?

But Tash had said he was here. Maybe he stopped

to wait for Noa to come to him. Yes, that must be it. He must be proud of her.

Noa kept walking. She lost track of the number of steps she'd taken. The hill rose.

Then her guiding staff plunged into empty space. She reeled back and nearly dropped her book.

"Daddy?" He had to be close, but there was no response.

Noa turned. "Arwen? Tash?" she called.

From down the hill, she thought she heard laughter. Mean laughter.

A sob broke from her chest, and tears spilled down her cheeks.

"Hello? Is anyone there?"

Nothing.

She felt around with her guiding staff. When it dropped into empty space again, she inched forward until it hit the flat of a step down and then fell off the next step. So she was at the top of a flight of stairs. But where was she?

Just a few blocks from home, she told herself. *I'm just a few blocks from home.* But it could have been miles. She only knew a few routes, and none of them had stairs. Even if she returned the way she'd come, how could she tell which house was hers? Panic buzzed in her ears. She didn't know where she was. She would be lost out here forever.

No. She took deep breaths, trying to stop crying. She hiccuped.

"Find the courage inside you," she whispered.

But she hadn't felt really brave for a long time. Not since the fever. The only time she'd felt strong was when her father cried over her mother, and she read to him, and he stopped.

She found the top step and sat, laying her guiding staff just behind her heels so she would know where it was. She set her book on her lap and opened it.

Her fingers were cold with fear, but she placed them on the page. And she read.

Cassian set out to find the dragons to restore his sight. He trusted in the gods to guide his quest. He followed the rising ground, for the dragons lived at the very peaks of the mountains.

Noa breathed raggedly, but the tears stopped, and her stomach unclenched.

Cassian walked for seven days and seven nights.

On the eighth day, he came to a patch of level ground, and for the first time he feared. He could not tell which way to go. He was lost, and he was alone.

"Just like me," Noa whispered.

Cassian almost lost hope. But if he despaired, he would be lost forever. He forced himself to calm down and think.

He was Cassian the strong. He had come this far. He could find his way forward.

She was Noa. She had learned so much. She could find her way home.

The peak of the mountain was north. It was morning. Cassian felt the heat of the sun on his right cheek. Right was east. Keeping the warmth to his right, he walked forward.

Noa marked her place and stood. She was trembling.

"Find the courage inside you." Fijen's voice boomed in her mind. "You have so much to share with the world, my child. And you know the way."

"I know the way," Noa said. "I do."

She would walk down the hill, using her guiding staff to stay to the right of the road. She would smell the bakery at the corner. She didn't need to see to find the way. She could do this.

Noa turned, lifted her face to the wind, and walked

home.

That night, Noa and her father finished *Cassian and the Dragon* together.

Cassian walked across the level rock to find the dragons waiting for him. Others had come seeking, they said, but they had never come alone, and they had never displayed such bravery. The dragons could not restore his sight. Those were only stories. But to commend his bravery, the young dragon Brighteyes said she would accompany Cassian down the mountain and become Cassian's companion. She would be his eyes. His friend.

"The End," Noa read.

"I'm so proud of you, Noa," her father said, kissing the top of her head. "You have no idea how proud I am."

She swallowed. It was hard to feel proud herself, hard to feel strong and brave, when her friends had betrayed her, when her mother had left her. Her father had said lots of people wouldn't understand, but she had not expected they would hurt her.

A small, hard, brave voice—not the goddess's voice, but a voice all her own—stood up and spoke in the back of her mind: *Then I'll show them. I'll teach* them *to see.*

A FIREFLY OF HOPE

by Alice Eakes

CW: Violence, discussions of rape and ableism, police

"I am still alive." I make myself say the words aloud. "I am still alive."

At this moment, I don't know if I want to be. Lying on the ground and falling asleep from hypothermia seems far easier than trying to reach other people, then telling anyone what just happened, then facing the consequences of what just happened. Just happened a minute ago. An hour ago. I don't know for sure. I might have lost consciousness. I might have simply shut my brain down to avoid the horror, the pain, the shame.

My bruised cheek pressed to the sand, I picture the consequences—accusations, arrest, the trial. Not mine, his. I may as well be on trial. I had read how women were treated—humiliated—but I will not back down. *Will. Not.* I think in one moment of clarity, of rage.

Or maybe I will lie here on the beach until some couple seeking privacy for a romantic tryst finds my frozen corpse.

The pain in my body will not allow me to sleep. The

pain in my body demands release other than sleep. *Help.* I need help. Or need to decide between acquiring help or remaining motionless between sea and civilization.

I begin to crawl before I realize my decision— creeping away from the gentle splash of water on the beach like a confused snail. My body's taking over my brain's control. Considering what I thought great a few hours earlier, shutting down my brain's function seems like a good idea. I ignore my heart as long as it continues to beat, also beyond control of my brain.

My foolish, treacherous brain. My foolish, treacherous heart.

"Do you want to go out with me tonight?" he asked at the end of homeroom.

Did I want to? I forced myself not to say "Yes" too quickly. After nearly a year of my longing for him to notice me, Dechlan Farrell noticed me in our two shared classes. A dream come true.

A nightmare in reality.

"Dress warmly," he told me, his voice low and husky, just short of gravelly. "We'll have a picnic."

I thought a picnic on the beach in November sounded romantic, not ridiculous. I thought because I knew him in school, part of a senior class that isn't more than a few hundred people, he couldn't be the sort of stranger with whom I should never be alone. He is seventeen like me, or maybe eighteen, but close in age.

Maybe he is close in other ways. Maybe he is close to my efforts to inch forward in search of the parking lot, then the road. Maybe he is in his car, watching, waiting, eager to see how the blind chick gets help.

Creeping through the sand toward what I hope is the parking lot, then the road, feels like trying to reach the top of a hill by going down. I think the sea is behind me but can't be a hundred percent sure. Sound plays funny tricks in open spaces like beaches. Though the tide is out, and the water near calm, it is loud enough to mask other sounds like traffic from the road or footfalls sneaking upon me. On the other hand, I might not be able to hear civilization because I am crawling parallel to the water and not away from it. If lights shine anywhere, I can't see them. Not since my retinas gave up working a year and a half ago.

So many bumbles this deterioration of my sight caused. Carrying cafeteria trays proved treacherous. I'd collided with someone who moved their chair out too far, and my bowls of soup and salad landed in his lap.

I miscounted rows of desks in the classroom and nearly sat on someone's lap. And so, the incidents occurred until I got oriented, adjusted, comfortable with a white cane and the need to ask for help once in a while.

No bumbles from my inability to see any longer were as bad as the one leaving me sobbing, staggering, then slipping into unconsciousness for a minute or an hour, on the beach after a date that wasn't a date, but a setup. I can ask for help without hesitation this time. If I find it. If I keep up my momentary momentum to find it.

If the cold doesn't sap my strength, my will, my determination. My hands and feet are numb. Somewhere I lost my shoes. Maybe he took them along with my jacket, my phone, my well-being.

I stop moving, listening. The distant hiss and gurgle of water against hardpacked sand comes through. Nothing else. The water seems farther away, as though I'd crawled some distance. Or maybe the tide receded farther. I have no way of knowing. I lie motionless again, until the distant beep of a car horn suggests a vehicle passing by. Maybe standing by.

Seeking help might lead to more horror.

I lurch forward and am sick, as though doing so can

rid my body and soul of Dechlan's assault.

"Say it like it is." I choke out the admission. "His rape."

Spoken aloud, the word shoots a bolt of energy through me. I stagger to my feet. My head spins from the blow he'd delivered to stop my fighting him. The sudden motion stirs the air, wafting his scent and mine around me—scent he left behind. Scent of stuff carrying his DNA.

Gagging, I double over—and strike my forehead on something solid. I cry out from renewed pain. My hand automatically seeks for the source of the collision. Cold concrete about a yard high. Round top. A parking bollard, one of the dozens keeping cars from driving onto the sand.

A spark flickers in my chest. Not enough fire for warmth. Not enough to call bravado. Yet something with more heat than the numbness. This replaces my spirit. A firefly of hope.

I grasp the bollard, leaning on it, waiting for the strength of mind and body to keep moving. I can follow the low, concrete posts around the lot for as far as they range. After that, I don't know. I can follow something.

I might also walk right into his car. He would like

that, laughing at me. I hear his laughter as though he stands beside me. "Why would you think I'd want you for anything more than to fuck you," he had mocked me when I said I didn't hookup on the first date.

I had never hooked up with anyone. I had yet to have the chance. Now the idea of allowing another man to touch me, to get close enough to touch me, leaves me doubled over the bollard, spitting bile onto the ground.

Weak, shaking, I stumble forward in search of the next bollard, and the next. Stones cut into my feet. Maybe broken glass, too. Pain slices my foot, and I cry out, then clap my hand over my mouth. No sound. I must make no sound. Dechlan needs to think I am still on the beach.

Four bollards. Five. Six. Seven. The line goes on. The night remains quiet. The sea is so far away, it seems more a memory than an enormous body of water. Maybe this is all the mere memory of a dream, a nightmare after all.

But then I lean on another post and catch that smell. Dreams don't have odours.

I reach for the next station. My reaching hand finds only air. The line of bollards has stopped. Those long, flat bumpers are now my guide. Beyond them, vegetation whispers in a light breeze.

"She… She… She…"

Between the concrete steps, I creep through paper bags and plastic cups, a can still harboring enough beer it squirts over my foot when I crush the can beneath my heel. Now I reek of cheap beer. People will think I was drinking. I did sometimes at parties, but not tonight. Dechlan brought vodka with some kind of flavouring. Cucumber. Nasty.

I kick the can aside and grope for the next concrete barrier. Nothing. My feet are so numb, I can feel nothing beneath them. I should bend and touch with my fingers. They are numb with cold too. So I move forward two steps, turn right for two steps, move two steps back. I fear I have drifted into the parking lot. I could wander there forever, until morning when more traffic travels the road to give me a landmark. Wander until I collapse from cold and exhaustion and pain.

I stand still to assess my surroundings, and that's when I hear the roar of an engine accelerating around a curve.

I am in the middle of the road.

The night is black. My clothes are black. My hair is

blond, pale enough to shine like a beacon. If the driver looks for beacons.

No one looks for anything on this road at night.

Frozen, unsure if right, left, or forward will take me off the road, I hold out my hands as though I can stop a ton of steel hurtling toward me. The roar of the engine grows louder, a beast lunging for its prey. But now I know which direction to run. Run if my feet co-operate. I think I'm pushing through Jell-O. My legs weigh hundreds of pounds apiece, and I lack the strength to propel these new tree-trunk thighs.

Tree trunks? Cut them up. Use them for firewood to warm me.

My peal of hysterical laughter is drowned out by the squeal of rubber on blacktop. The roar settles to a purr. Heat radiates to my right side. I reach and encounter the grill of a radiator. The car stopped no more than a foot from me.

Air escapes my lungs and won't come back. I gasp and gasp and gasp and nothing gets past my constricted throat.

Then a door opens. "What the fuck are you doing in the middle of the road," demands a voice roughened by too many cigarettes. I can smell the smoke wafting from the car. "Trying to get yourself—do you need help?" The tone changed in midstream from angry to gentle.

"Please," I say with the few trickles of oxygen that have managed to squeeze into my chest. "Please."

From tree trunks, my legs become canned green beans, and I collapse on the road.

The next six hours pass in a blur of mortification. Cotton swabs invade my body. Needles are jammed into my veins. And always, questions probe into my head.

"How did you get hit on the head?"

"How did you cut your feet?"

"Where are the rest of your clothes?"

My answers are simple. "He hit me."

"I don't know."

"I don't know."

They didn't make me wait in the waiting room but took me to a private space at once. That was the best part of the night.

"Have you been drinking?" a nurse asks me.

"No," I answer.

Dechlan drank something strong, like whisky. I remember smelling it on his breath as he—

I am sick on the floor. I know somewhere in the room an emesis bowl probably sits on a table, but I have no way of knowing where it is. More humiliation. More embarrassment.

This is when I begin to cry. The sobs are hard and gasping, painful in my aching head, revealing injuries to my chest I didn't know about until it heaved up and down so hard I couldn't get my breath.

And this is when my parents walk into the room.

"What have you done to my daughter?" I hear Mom's voice rushing toward me.

"No, ma'am, you can't touch her yet," a nurse who sounds like she doubles as a drill sergeant says. "We aren't finished with the forensic exam."

"Have the police been contacted?" Of course my father would ask that. He is a journalist on the crime beat, and this is a potential story. A big one with primary sources.

Blind girl attacked on beach.

"Dad, Mom, please." My voice is weak. I don't know

if they hear me. "Go away."

Going through the exam is humiliating enough without my parents watching.

"But, Maddie," Mom cries, "we're here to support you."

I turn my face away from them, the bruise on my cheek aching at the pressure against the thin hospital pillow. "Help by going away."

"Mr. and Mrs. Donavan," the nurse says, "we are doing our job. I have special training in dealing with these cases—"

"My daughter is not a case," Mom cries. "She's a person."

"And we are trying to maintain her humanity the best we can," the nurse says, her voice too loud, but not unkind. "Now, please, wait outside the room so we can finish."

"The police," Dad reiterates.

The room door closes. No one answers his question.

The interlude with my parents has given me time to calm myself. As though the crying jag drained emotions from my soul, I am numb. I feel the pokes and prods of the nurse and then a doctor performing further indignities on my body, but I feel nothing in my heart.

I experience no embarrassment when the nurse takes away my clothes right down to my underpants, knowing some forensic specialist will be collecting evidence from them.

So, when I do face the cops—a detective, he tells me—I can say with perfect calm, "Dechlan Farrell did this to me. He took me to the beach and raped me."

Someone gasped. Of course it's Mom. I'm still a minor, so they are in the room, admonished to be quiet.

"How do you know it's Mr. Farrell who did this?" the detective asks.

I stare at him. Okay, I can't see him, but my eyebrows and lids respond as though I can stare in astonishment.

"What do you mean?" I ask. "I was with him."

"But can you be sure he was the one who assaulted you?" the detective asks. "Did you see him?"

As quickly as the numbness descended upon me, it evaporates in a flame of rage. I surge to my feet, hands gripping the edge of the table. "Are you saying because I'm blind I can't know who I was with?"

"Yes, Maddie, that's exactly what I'm saying," responds the detective.

I want to punch him. I want to shove the table so

hard into his solar plexus that he can't breathe.

I know the truth, but who is going to believe me?

"My daughter is not clueless," Mom says. "If she says she was with Dechlan Farrell, then she was with Dechlan Farrell."

"Did you see him pick her up for this date?" asks the detective.

Silence from the parent gallery.

They weren't at home when I left. Mom was at parent-teacher conferences, as she's a schoolteacher, and Dad was still chasing down some story before his deadline.

"Furthermore," the detective continues, "just because she left with Mr. Farrell doesn't mean she stayed with him. She wouldn't be the first young lady who left with one boy and ended up hooking up with another."

"Hooking up?" Mom's voice reached a pitch every dog in town must have heard. "My daughter does not hook up with boys."

"She doesn't even date much," Dad said in an undertone.

Not because I am lacking in looks, or so my best friend, Isabella, tells me. But a popular boy once declared that only a loser would go out with a blind girl because he couldn't do any better.

So, I guess the detective's skepticism is understandable. Dechlan Farrell is not a loser. He is a nice boy. He's a good student and a tennis champion, not some macho football player known for his misogyny.

I turn to my parents. "Take me home. I have nothing more to say to these people."

I have nothing more to say to anyone. Finally allowed to shower, I scrub and scrub until the water turns cold, then I crawl into my bed, ignore the cup of tea Mom has brought me, but take the sleeping pill the doctor offered. I want to sleep. I want to escape. I want to wake up knowing nothing worse can ever happen to me.

But I'm wrong. Worse can happen.

Next day, when I'm trying not to wake up, the detective pays us a visit to inform me that Dechlan could not have been the person who assaulted me. He was with his friends, who all vouch for his presence with them. I am labelled as either a liar with some score to settle against Dechlan, or too inept—due to my blindness—to know who I was with on a beach picnic in the middle of November.

"Evidence on the beach?" I ask the detective.

"Tide washed anything away, if you were even there," the ass responds.

"If—" I choke on my objection.

"The hospital said her clothes were full of sand," Dad says.

"And so was her hair," Mom adds.

"Then she was at the beach sometime during the evening." I can hear the shrug in the detective's voice.

"But there has to be some kind of evidence," Dad says. "DNA, for instance."

"No cause to request DNA samples from Mr. Farrell since he has an alibi."

The detective takes his leave soon after. I tell my parents I'm fine, but I'm not; I am sick to my stomach.

But not as sick as when I log onto social media in my room. The posts on my timeline are vile, misogynistic, ableist, just plain mean. They all sum up to the same thing—Dechlan had no need to go out with me. He could get half the girls in school. None of his other dates complained about him. I must have egged him on, then decided to take revenge when he wasn't interested.

That latter makes no sense at all. I have DNA from him. Or rather, the cops do. If I can't prove it with my hearing and knowledge, then I have to prove it with science.

If I can bear to return to school.

Mom and Dad let me stay out for the week. They get my homework from my teachers, who seem to think I've suffered some kind of mental breakdown.

"Perhaps public school is too much for her," my AP history teacher suggests to my parents.

"She has the highest grade in the class," Mom points out. "How could public school be too much for her?"

Mom fumes, but I'm too worn down to care. I shut down my social media accounts, though lots of people email me. Two things stand out in the emails. One is a question—asking how it feels to be "gangbanged"—and the other is that I hear nothing from my supposed best friend, Isabella.

The latter somehow hurts more than Dechlan's assault. Isabella and I have been friends for six years. I can't believe she's abandoned me when I need a friend the most.

The former point leaves me shaking my head, bemused. I never said I was gangbanged. Dechlan was the only one who assaulted me. Only Dechlan. And I remember little enough of that due to the blow on my head.

The blow, apparently that is also working against me. I was knocked out. I imagined it all in a concussion dream. I wandered down the road in my state of confusion. Maybe my concussion left me imagining a fantasy so clearly that I thought it happened.

More nonsense theories. For one, I didn't have a concussion. Shock more than head injury, a doctor for follow-up tells me, is why I don't remember a lot of details.

By the end of the week, I wish I'm not in the middle of my senior year. Otherwise, I would have asked my parents to use some of my college fund to put me into a private school. Too late now. I have to stick it out despite how people treat me.

I intend to go back to school the next Monday. A week has passed since the assault. The emails have slowed down. Maybe everyone will just ignore me. I'm not sure I can manage the idea of being taunted to my face. It's not allowed at school, of course, but I've seen how others are treated, those who are considered odd or freaky or too bad to be cool. Teachers manage to hear very little when they choose. With me, because everyone likes Dechlan, I'm all too likely to spawn the teachers' inability to hear the bullying.

If only I was not about to walk the path alone. If only I had Isabella at my side, a faithful friend. She, however, has ghosted me. She can't text or call. My phone is probably out to sea somewhere. She could email, though, and hasn't. My emails to her have gone unread.

On Saturday, Dad brings me a new phone. It's the latest accessible one—accessible from the manufacturer—and easy for me to use with the phone reading the screen. I have a different number.

"Figured you didn't want texts you don't need," Dad said in a gruff voice.

After thanking him, I text Isabella... and get no response. Nothing. I shut myself into my room and listen to death metal until Mom comes in to ask if I would be okay if she and Dad keep a dinner date with some friends.

"Of course," I say.

The idea of being alone is priceless. Mom cares, but she has hovered so much, I expect to hear the whirr of helicopter blades around her. Without her around, I can lose myself in a movie with audio description of the action or listen to a book without being interrupted every fifteen minutes with offers of tea, cocoa, or food. I haven't been eating enough, I guess, and food turns my stomach. The last meal I ate was with Dechlan on the beach. Deli sandwiches and chips that tasted wonderful at the time. Now the smell of bread makes me want to puke.

I tell Mom and Dad not to worry about me and have a nice evening. This has been a stressful week for them too. They didn't ask for such trouble. Maybe they have gotten pushback or scorn from friends and colleagues they aren't telling me about. Their daughter the slut, the whore, the liar like that girl in the magazine that turned out to be false.

Except she claimed a whole frat house or something raped her. I only knew of one, Dechlan Farrell, the boy whose DNA I must collect—somehow.

I need help with this. If only I have her to help...

And suddenly a ping interrupts the movie I'm watching. *I'm at your back door*, says the text.

I scramble for the kitchen and there she is: Isabella with open arms. She's half a head taller than I am, so she pushes my face onto her shoulder so I can cry. It's the first time I have since the night it happened. She says nothing until I stop sobbing, then she finds me a wad of tissues and makes us tea, as comfortable in our kitchen as she is in her own. She talks while she fills the teakettle and puts bags into mugs.

"I'm so sorry I haven't been here for you. My mom wouldn't let me come. She had a hair appointment on Saturday at the same time Dechlan's mom had one, and the woman convinced everyone her son never took you out. She said he was with his friends because they all came back to the house together and ate her out of house and home."

"So, she wouldn't let you come around me," I guess.

"Threatened me with grounding till Christmas Day if I did."

"Then why are you here now?" I was happy to have her here but didn't want her to miss all the holiday activities because of me.

"She's on some women's retreat."

The kettle whistled, stopped. Water splashed into cups. The aroma of mint and chamomile filled the kitchen.

"There you go." She sets the cup on the table in front of me, then pulls out a chair. "And Dad couldn't have me go to his house this weekend because he's got a new girlfriend, so I've been trusted to stay alone."

"And snuck out to see me." My eyes fill again. "I thought... I was afraid you... Believed all the things..."

"Thanks for trusting me." Her tone is sarcastic. "I know you're telling the truth about Dechlan. No one will say anything around me because they know we're friends, but I still hear things."

"Hear... what?" Stomach twisting between excitement and anxiety, I grip my mug with both hands, hoping the warmth will calm me.

"This is hard." Isabella sips her tea. "I mean, maybe I should wait until your parents are home."

I'm shaking now, bile rising in my throat from apprehension. "Please," is all I can get past my throat.

"It's ugly, Maddie. I hope you're getting therapy or something."

"I start next week. But why... what are people saying now? Surely it can't be worse than what's been said already."

"It is." Isabella takes a deep breath. "Maddie?" She wraps her hands around mine. "Maddie, do you think you could have been, um, assaulted by more than one guy?"

"More than one?" I say, sounding stupid.

My mind flashes back to the cold, hard sand, pounded down by the waves. I remember a hand on my zipper, another up my shirt. I twisted. I flailed with my fists. I tried to kick. Then the blow came, and the world spun out of reality until I came to with hot breath smelling of beer blowing across my face.

Dechlan hadn't been drinking beer.

I barely make it to the bathroom in time. Isabella follows to hold my hair back, then gets me a cold washcloth to sponge the cold sweat from my face, and a glass of water. Neither of us speaks again until we are back at the kitchen table.

"So Dechlan *was* with his friends," I croak through a raw throat.

"It was a bet that went too far," Isabella says. "That's what Asher told Hector when they were drunk the other night."

Asher Brown, one of Dechlan's friends kicked off the tennis team for his drinking, and Hector Ruiz, one of his drinking buddies.

A bet gone wrong. A bet gone too far. I am worth as much as a pack of cards on a dealer's table.

Darkness slips through me like a poisonous heavy

metal, weighing me down, threatening to carry me all the way to the end. It's seductive, that blackness. I can slip into oblivion and forget what happened, forget this new information.

And these guys will get away with hurting me. If they do, who knows who they'll hurt next? Maybe someone like Isabella, without two supportive parents or the resources to pay for therapy.

"They will not win," I declare in a voice as cold as the sand left hard and still behind the tide. "I will get these fuckers if it's the last thing I do."

Isabella is a rock at my side on Monday morning. She meets me at Mom's car when I arrive at school, then she walks with me: me applying my white cane to navigate, her brushing our arms once in a while so I know she is close if I need to grab hold of someone. Although I hear dozens of conversations along the sidewalk leading to the school, they fall silent as we pass. If their eyes were sparks, I know I would be ablaze by now.

About halfway along the silent gauntlet, I want to turn and run. My steps falter. My cane catches in a crack in the sidewalk, tripping me, and someone snickers. My chest tightens. I can't breathe.

"Keep going," Isabella murmurs. Then, when I still hesitate between forward and running away, she says one word to galvanize me, "DNA."

DNA. If I am not in the cafeteria during lunch, I might not get a chance to acquire Dechlan and company's DNA.

I move forward. The doors are open despite the cold. Odours of mildew and sweat and too much body spray swirl toward me. Familiar. Not frightening. These people can't cause me any lasting harm. Nearly the worst has already happened to me. Their words will hurt, but not for long if my plan is successful.

The whispered jeers sting for the time being, though. I've never been called any of the things they accuse me of. If anything, I've been considered too much a goodie by students and teachers alike. I never got in trouble for talking in class, even though I could be as gabby as anyone else. My accusation against a popular boy seems to have changed all that. One extreme to the other. Maybe, when the truth comes out, something in the middle and true range will emerge. I can hope.

If I succeed.

Isabella walks me to my locker, then my first class. She has to leave me there at the door, as her scheduled class is at the other end of the building. I'm okay in the first class.

But Dechlan is in my second period class. He doesn't speak to me, but someone thumps on my desk as they pass. I suspect it's him. Seems like a childish thing to do. At the end of class I try to pick up my electronic notetaker and find it's stuck to the desk with a huge wad of gum.

Super childish prank.

I pretend not to notice. Lots of people think I don't know what's up with anything anyway, so I play into this. Mostly I try to navigate as normally as possible, but today, I need to play up the bumbling, unaware blind girl. I can bear some humiliation over my disability if the end works.

Third and fourth period go as well as can be expected. The teachers don't call on me. Maybe, like most everyone else, they're pretending I'm not there. It's not the first time I've been made to feel invisible.

Then lunchtime arrives. I hate the cafeteria. It's so loud, I can get disoriented easily. Isabella or someone from the school choir I sing in, usually lends me a hand. Today, I pretend I have no one. In truth, Isabella is giving me directions through a Bluetooth headphone stuck in one ear and connected to my phone. I get into the line. Someone says, "Without your guide dog today?" Not the first time Isabella has been called this. She usually plays it up. Today, I ignore the asshole.

At the counter, I order food I'm too nervous to eat. But I need a tray to carry, and it can't be empty. Loaded tray balanced on one hip, cane in my other hand, I head back to the dining area.

"He's in the first row of tables next to the windows," Isabella says in my ear.

Great. I have to walk nearly the entire width of the cafeteria. The noise level seems twice its normal volume. I'd have preferred that morning's hush on the sidewalk, but apparently I'm no longer interesting. That's a good thing. I don't want Dechlan noticing me coming.

"You're nearly there," Isabella says. "Okay, turn right and... now!"

What I accidentally did so often when I first lost my

sight, I now do on purpose. I bump my tray into someone just enough to tilt it, so its contents slide into that person's lap. Iced tea, soup, and a greasy grilled cheese sandwich

"Watch where you're going, bitch," Dechlan shouts.

He leaps to his feet, still yelling. Others are yelling too. Chairs scrape along the floor, indicating others have shot to their feet. Liquid splashes. I stand still, looking, I hope, bewildered and helpless.

"Got it," Isabella crows beside me. "Let's go."

Isabella grabs my arm. I toss my tray into the chaos behind me and, for the first time, let her lead me by holding onto me. No time to waste, we switch positions to me holding her arm. In a moment, one of the guys with Dechlan and the man himself might figure out what we were up to and give chase. Thus far, all that follows us is their nasty name-calling.

We duck into the girl's bathroom outside the cafeteria door and huddle together in the extra-large stall. There, we tuck three plastic bottles into paper bags and Isabella labels them with the right names, easy to do since each had been drinking something different.

"I got video too," Isabella says. "Just so we can

prove where we got these bottles."

The cops might not have enough evidence to request DNA from Dechlan and company, but I don't need a warrant. It will cost me a fortune, but I can have these bottles tested for DNA and then, I know without a doubt, without sight, it will match Dechlan Farrell's, as well at least two of his friends.

My firefly of hope is now a torch of victory.

HEROIC DREAMS

by Randy Lacey

As it often does on a hot and humid summer's evening, the storm raged on in the small central Alberta town of Trochu. The thunder boomed through the desolate streets, rattling walls and scaring young children and their pets. The air was heavily charged with ion particles being released from the unrelenting lightning. That was not all that was in the air this night. If one had been listening closely during the cacophony of thunderclaps and flashes of lightning, one might have also heard the whispers of murder in the air.

The house sat on a corner lot, a stone's throw from the downtown core. It was not a big house from the outward appearance, but it sat larger than some of the other houses close by. It stood on a double lot, which should have made the house appear smaller. The proximity of the other smaller houses gave the house its stature. There was a wooden deck at the front of the house with four steps that led up to the main entrance. The exterior light shone dimly in the dense darkness that had come in with the storm. As a light source, it failed in its duty to illuminate, which was unfortunate for Danny Meehan.

Danny had lived in the house for over twenty years. He and his son, Lee, had purchased it together. His son only used the residence as a fixed address, as he worked on the road more often than not. When on occasion he wasn't on the road, he stayed with his father and their cat, CeCe. As long as he had lived in this house, there existed what he called an open-door policy. Simply put, it meant that all were welcome without invitation, for any reason, at any time. Few people took him up on the anytime option, for which he was truly grateful.

Local youth would often come by just to hang out. Younger kids, who felt that they were being bullied or scared would come by seeking a safe place to be. Even seniors wanting to talk over a cup of coffee would frequent the house. The only rule Danny had was that you knock before you walked in, then identify yourself once inside. For you see, Danny was blind. Not totally blind, but the vision he did have didn't allow him to see much detail or colour.

At the exact moment a flash of lightning lit up the night sky, which gave it a momentary appearance of daylight, the front door to Danny's home opened. A shadowy figure went in, unnoticed by anyone in the house or around it. The door was quietly closed, and the only interior light visible was the soft fluorescent glow above the kitchen sink. Somewhere in the house, the faint sound of AC/DC's "Thunderstruck" could be heard. The unknown visitor stealthily moved their way through the house. The cat who had been sleeping on the sofa awoke and gave a soft meow as it stretched. A barely audible voice emanated from behind a doorway. It was a muffled admonition to the cat to go back to sleep.

The stranger paused momentarily in the centre of the living room and surveyed the room. There was not much of value that could be seen. Looking in the direction of the doorway, they spotted a faint light. A periodic flash from perhaps a computer screen or a television danced through the doorway, giving it an eerie glow. The stranger concluded it was a computer monitor. Another AC/DC song came on, this time it was "Jailbreak," and Danny began to sing along to it. *Poorly,* the stranger thought. He slowly crept towards the door, being careful not to make any sudden noises.

Without warning, a whoosh just missed the

stranger's head, then something solid connected with the doorframe. Before he could move towards Danny, another whoosh, and a thud against his head. It had knocked him back through the doorway into the living room.

"Who are you? What do you want?" Danny shouted. Not waiting for an answer, he added, "There's nothing of value in the house."

He listened for any noise that would betray the stranger's whereabouts. He heard nothing.

Danny steadied the wooden practice katana, waiting for any sound that gave away the intruder's location. Reaching for the keyboard on his desk, he fumbled for the appropriate key and muted the music. He stood inside his office just behind a high-standing dresser. Slowly, he pushed his leather office chair towards the doorway, hoping to block it. The wheels scratched along the wood laminate flooring, giving away his intentions. He released the chair, pushing it away from him towards the door. As quick as he heard the chair hitting the door frame, he heard it rolling back towards him even quicker than he'd sent it. He swung wildly and connected with the dresser.

His hands vibrated upon contact and felt the

reverberation crawl up his arms in a wave of pain that instantly flooded his eyes with tears. As he was contending with the pain, the stranger pounced upon him, knocking him backwards into the desk. The monitor on the top shelf rocked with the impact. It teetered on the edge before settling down in place. Danny struggled to get free from the bear hug he now found himself in. His breath had been knocked out of him, and he was trying to recover. The unknown assailant tightened his grip around Danny's torso, not giving his lungs much room to expand. Danny felt himself fading, passing out.

The first glass of water had failed to snap Danny out of his unconscious state. The second one however, jolted him awake. Realizing that his arms and legs were bound, he wiggled in frustration. Danny felt a gentle tapping against his left ear. He presumed it was the practice sword. The taps steadily got harder until it caused his ear to sting. Then it began on the right ear. He tried to move his head to prevent it, but with every adjustment, the hits got harder. He stopped fighting it, and the hitting ceased.

"Who are you?" Danny asked in a defeated whisper.

"Let's see if you can figure it out for yourself," the stranger said. "Shall we play a game of twenty questions then? Go ahead, ask away."

Danny sat quietly in defiance of this stranger's taunting. He was determined not to play along. He could hear the storm raging on outside and knew it would be pointless to scream.

A tap on his ear, and another. Slightly harder this time.

"Okay, okay! Have we met before?" Danny inquired.

"A long time ago," came the response.

"Did we meet in Alberta?"

There was a long, drawn-out sigh before the stranger hissed a "no" in response.

Danny continued asking his questions. If he were to believe the stranger was answering truthfully, he was almost certain he knew who it was, but wasn't sure why. He was about to change the line of questioning when he sensed the stranger had inched closer, almost touching Danny.

There was a loud clap of thunder.

The power must have gone out because Danny could now hear all the electronics re-initializing. The answering machine and the computer were booting back up. Seizing his opportunity, Danny stood up quickly and rushed forward towards his captor, pushing him hard into the doorframe with his shoulder to the gut. The stranger was winded and had collapsed to the floor. Danny shook his legs free from the loosely tied strings around his legs and began to kick at his uninvited guest.

Danny was awakened by the dry, scratchy licking of CeCe's tongue on his ear. Danny lazily scratched behind CeCe's ear while he himself let out a deep sigh.

"Even in my dreams I can be the hero," he said to the already again sleeping cat.

HOW IS IT YOU SING?

by Niki White

CW: Grief

I cannot believe I'm here: actually inside the music building on my college campus. That my ears have just been vigorously assaulted by a trombone doesn't help my already sour, rebellious mood. *No, no, by all means, blow your high F while someone's walking by; it's not like you have control over the instrument.* I give the thing an echoing thwack with my cane, receiving a knee-jerk response of "sorry" from the trombonist, who's completely oblivious to my little revenge.

"It's fine," I mumble automatically, tiredly, because I know since he's a sightie—sighted person— encountering an obviously blind person, he's apologizing for being in my way. My ringing ears will probably never occur to him.

I slouch past the inconsiderate musician into my classroom, noting, as my cane suddenly glides smoothly across the floor with little thudding whispers as the tip bumps against the cracks—a sound akin to a roller skate on a rink—that it's wooden. The reverberating hiss of the air vents above also tells me this room possesses a high ceiling. Kudos to the architect for an acoustically appropriate space that will ensure we can all tell whether someone's really good, okay, or an embarrassment to themselves.

I grudgingly allow that it's better than a carpeted room, as I wander aimlessly in search of a chair. Granny used to say carpet sucked the soul out of a song.

I dig my fingers into the rubber grip of my cane hard enough to make it hurt, but it's clearly a pointless distraction. My mind goes right along and drudges up how she'd been the only person who understood my fury that year the practice room was carpeted, and I'd been forced to rely even more stringently on my—

No. I can't think about that. Won't.

My cane hits something that sounds plastic, but echoes slightly. I reach out and my fingers make contact with the smooth varnished wooden front of a piano. The air around me feels closed, which indicates the front of the room in spaces like this. Typically, classrooms and lecture halls have a different front-of-the-room feel.

The sweeps of my cane become overly wide swings in an even more pitifully transparent attempt to keep me in the here and now, giving a bad name to prior orientation and mobility instructors in my desperation. *Sorry guys, I'll do you proud when there are people around to see my cane skills. Promise.*

The clink of the tip against metal thankfully jolts me completely from my train of thought, and after confirming the object's a chair, I drag it to the approximate centre of the room. After stowing my things underneath the hard metal seat (with the exception of the folder containing my sheet music the class was emailed to bring in), there's nothing left for me to do but wait and ponder how I'm going to get back at Miranda for this.

It's the second semester in a row I've been cursed with her, the nosiest roommate on the planet, and how she was left alone with my overly chatty seven-year-old sister Katie, I'll never know. I don't care if I'm allergic, I'm getting a guide dog next year, then I can get a single.

But apparently, Miranda mentioned I had a pretty singing voice (curse you catchy, meaningless, barely-ever-logically-rhymed pop music), which led Katie to expound upon the boxed-up awards at my parents' house with my name and titles of vocal competitions on them. I don't know if she explained that I haven't actually sung in three years, but Miranda should've been content with the mystery being solved—I'd always stopped my accidental humming if she commented on it or I caught myself at it. But somehow, maybe because Miranda thinks that since I'm yoked to so much technology I'll comply to anything on a screen, she put this information into her selfish little head and decided to fill the last free space on my schedule with a musical theatre workshop.

"You would have been wait-listed for the classes you wanted anyway," Miranda had lectured.

I could make none of the comebacks I'd wanted to with Katie still in the room, so settled for the logical rebuttal. "Good point, but I don't want to be in theatre. I'm a terrible actor."

"But you're a great singer, so things will balance out."

"That's very sweet. A girl could get a cavity standing next to you. But you don't know I'm a great singer; you know I'm a decent singer and are relying on hearsay."

"What's hearsay?" Katie asked.

"What you hear someone else say."

"Oh! That makes sense. But I'm not 'someone.'"

"I know you're not, Katie cat, but—"

"I was helping you, Tracy."

"Sure," I'd said dryly, turning my head towards Miranda's voice, "because usually when I help someone, I wait until they go to the bathroom to act on their behalf."

The obvious solution to all of this would have been for me to change it. But my mom (back too late from the car with the last box of my stuff) had responded to Katie's pronouncement of, "Tracy's taking a singing class!" by giving me a hug and saying how Granny would be so happy, and she'd known I wouldn't just turn my back on thirteen years of voice lessons. Plus, when the family had gone, Miranda refused to turn on the talking program that makes my computer—and thereby my schedule—accessible to me.

So, blindsided (no pun intended), manipulated, unintentionally guilted, and curious in the way you're curious about the details of a car accident to know just how deluded or pretentious my classmates would be, it was inevitable that I'd come for the first class. Of course, I'll be dropping it at the end of the week, and telling my flighty cohabitant (and Mom and Katie) that the workshop just wasn't what I'd thought it would be, so ultimately, I win.

The door opens, followed by footsteps clacking on the wood and a screech of a chair being pulled up to the left of mine.

"Uh, if you don't mind my asking," a girl's voice pipes up, "did someone help you with the chair?"

Maybe it's because I'm already on edge, but the abrupt question rubs me the wrong way.

It's a common enough association for some sighties that blind equals helpless, and usually I'm cool with explaining where this view's flawed. But seriously? That's the first thing out of this girl's mouth? No "Hi, I'm blah blah. What did you bring in for Professor Harper to get a sense of your voice?" but instead, "Are you as needy as I presume you are from stereotypical generalizations and what-I-believe-are-true representations in movies?"

I'm dropping on principle now.

"Yeah," I say sweetly. "Whoever put the piano at the front of the room helped me get oriented, and whoever decided classroom air vents should almost always be placed a little to the right of the ceiling's centre helped me navigate."

Silence, and the me that would've answered

differently—politely—in any other class feels a little guilty. Then a perky, "I'm Amanda!"

"Tracy." *And please get the hint that I don't want to chit-chat.*

"How are you?" Amanda gushes, then ploughs on before I've even opened my mouth. "Because I'm feeling sick and want to go home."

"Fine, though I agree about the going home part."

Okay, that had all the politeness of a stampeding elephant; try again, Trace. "I'm sure your nerves will clear up," I say after a beat (great, now I'm thinking musically), unsure that it matters whether or not I contribute to the conversation.

"So, what are you singing?" Amanda asks, sounding more like the kindergarten teacher who tries to tempt the shy kid into playing than a nervous girl.

"Now what would be the fun in telling you when we have to make introductions," I answer dully.

"Oh yeah!" She falls blessedly silent after this stunningly witty comeback, and I feel a sharper twinge of guilt. I shouldn't be taking my anger and uneasiness at being here out on her. What if she's new?

If she is, she'll soon know I wasn't lying about the intros; standard, "Hello/good afternoon/good morning, my name is… and I will be singing/performing…" The divas in these workshops adore these moments; waiting to see if they know the song, whether or not their classmate mimics some famous name whose made the piece what it is today, makes it their own, or is merely the latest person to sing it note for note with no feeling whatsoever. Because it's not bad enough that the only thing for an entire classroom of either opinionated, or nervous, or cocky, or hijacked—okay, that last one probably only applies to me—people to do is hang off your every word. They have to judge you, too.

The room quickly fills up, and Amanda finds others to chatter with. I don't really pay attention again until a woman's voice says, "I see you all got my email. Good. Now, how many of you have been in a musical theatre workshop before?"

Apparently, I'm not the only one to raise my hand (it was during a summer when my voice teacher was playing the fairy godmother in a production of *Cinderella*), because Professor Harper murmurs, "Okay, a couple of you. Well, because this class is about performing, we're just going to jump right in. The songs you brought in today will be the songs you work on for at least a quarter of this semester, unless you've brought in something strictly to show off, in which case you'll be picking something else that can challenge you at least marginally." This gets a laugh. "This way you'll already have a song you hopefully enjoy singing, and one that's already completely memorized, so half the battle will be over.

"Now when you finish, I'll be giving you a few comments on how to improve your performance, which I do want you to work on for next week, but please don't take these too seriously. All of you will have something to improve on."

With that, she takes roll, introduces the pianist, Erik (who arrives after six of the nine names have been confirmed present), and has us stand where we are to sing a few warm-ups. They consist of vowel exercises (the five sounds A, E, I, O and U, sung on three notes both up and down the scale) and lip trills (blowing out air so that your lips pucker up and vibrate like a kid making a motor sound as they play with cars). Peers who aren't loud are probably self-conscious, or struggle with the lip exercise, producing either loud puffs of air or spitting sounds that probably contain saliva in their frustration.

After about ten minutes of that, we're told to sit back down and asked if anyone feels brave enough to go first. Only the hissing air vents respond to the gauntlet Professor Harper has thrown down, which is fine by me. I'm rattled—those warm-ups were supposed to be more challenging, damn it!—and rooting for this class to be a bunch of wallflowers; the more time's taken up by silence, the less time we'll have to get through everyone.

The prospect of dropping the workshop without ever having to sing a note is thrilling, and one I hadn't considered.

"I will," says a nasal male voice, and I wonder how bad a person it makes me for imagining thwacking him the way I did the trombone.

"Lovely," Professor Harper replies, "Hand over your music to Erik, and before you start, tell us your name and what you'll be singing. Just those two things. Nothing about the song."

His name is Travis, and unfortunately, he'll be singing Stephen Sondheim's "Not While I'm Around," a beautiful musical theatre piece about a boy wanting to protect his guardian from a character who he thinks is a villain. I say unfortunately, because Travis sings the way he talks, in a nasal whine that mangles the melody, makes certain words unclear, and turns the high notes into cat yowls.

When he's done, and we've applauded stiffly, Professor Harper goes through some pronunciation exercises with him that get his lyrics out of the nose somewhat. This means he has to hold his nose a lot, and the song regains some of the sweetness Sondheim intended. I guess Travis makes other people think they have nothing to be nervous about, because the next person to take to the floor is Amanda.

Her song fits the rude chatterbox impression I've formed of her—Stephen Schwartz's "Popular" is a shallowly-worded piece wherein a popular girl sings about how she can help an unpopular girl conform—but Amanda either cannot or has not learned to support the sound by using her diaphragm. When you do, breathing in so that your stomach fills with air, your ribs expand (and stay expanded until you take your next breath), and all the muscles below your belly button contract (that includes the main pelvic one), you can actually sound as loud as you would with the help of a microphone if you wanted to.

I can tell she isn't doing this, because Amanda

sounds not only like she's talking at a regular volume, but is running out of air scarily fast throughout the bouncy, bubblegum tune. Erik kindly waits for her to pant and gasp in lungfuls of air so she can continue, but the comedy that's the crux of the song is lost by the time she finishes.

Professor Harper starts sorting this out by having her press her stomach against a wall, keeping it out and resisting against the hard surface so nothing falls in on itself. If it sounds like hard going, that's because it is, and Amanda sounds tired and winded when they're through.

Next up (called from the roster, because I guess people are starting to feel daunted now) are four girls and one guy who sing respective Disney songs ("A Dream is a Wish Your Heart Makes," "Just Around the Riverbend," "Belle Reprise," "Someday My Prince Will Come," and "Be Prepared"). The characters represented by the four female soloists are all known for having beautiful and immediately recognizable voices, so the girls try their best to mimic the professional singers found on the original movie soundtracks. The villain's vocal classification is just a touch too low for the student trying to pull it off.

Professor Harper talks a lot to the girls about ways to make the pieces their own, emphasizing different words and showcasing different emotions than the originators: "Because if someone wants to hear someone sounding exactly like the original Belle, they won't hold auditions, they'll just hire the original Belle."

The guy gets information about changing his song's register, so he can sing the low notes more like a human and less like a dying car battery, and the trio of student, professor, and pianist spend some time finding out what vocal type he actually is—more handsome prince material than dastardly villain. I don't think he's pleased with this fact, but maybe he doesn't know just how many songs are available to him.

Professor Harper clearly has a rapport with the penultimate student, because instead of saying another name when the Reluctant Prince Charming sits back down, she quips, "Back for more internal pain?"

"I'm a music major. Life is pain," a male voice returns, with just enough of a mock-melodramatic tone to draw a few giggles from every female student but me—and Professor Harper. Their mirth lasts longer than the joke warranted, so apparently, he's attractive. I'm waffling about whether to classify him as the truly pretentious peer ("Princey" would have filled that slot before this guy opened his mouth), but then he gives the title of his piece.

Unless you want to humiliate yourself years after the workshop has ended—because no one will forget you butchering a gorgeously passionate, musically strenuous song where the singer's required to be two people in a fatal struggle—you save a masterpiece like Frank Wildhorn's "The Confrontation" for the end of the semester. The breath control that was Amanda's problem has to be so precise that performers have been known to record one or the other parts, so the audience doesn't witness an onstage burnout.

As Erik plays the opening notes and chords, I'm betting I'll know exactly where he'll slip up, but am distracted, due to being enveloped in the warm cocoon of melody pouring out of Golden Tenor guy's mouth. He soon changes from emoting love, grief, and desperation to the harsh back-and-forth of the dueling charismatic men, but the shift doesn't break the spell he initially wrought. He has the type of voice that, if he knows what he's doing (and does he ever!), causes shivers down the spine (and more discrete places), earns awards, and makes you think that as long as this voice sang about world domination, you'd be willing to hear it out.

According to Professor Harper, who puts up a good pretense of being unmoved (I can tell by the slight hitch in her breath before she critiques, though she's given time to pull herself back to a professional-versus-audience demeanor while applause and cries of "Dude!" pervade the air), he keeps his jaw too taut. By the time they've made some progress in getting it to hang motionless throughout the first verse, freeing up the sound even more, I can tell the class is unwilling to applaud, unwilling to acknowledge that the work (for now) has come to an end.

I, meanwhile, am swallowing tears, knowing in my gut there was a time when I too could sing with such technical purity and emotional abandon, but unable to pinpoint precisely when. It saddens and terrifies me, until a nasty little voice in my head begins to stir, and I rein it back.

"And last but not least, Tracy McDonnily," Professor Harper proclaims, the quickest to shake off any stupor she's been left in. "Do you need help getting—"

"I got it."

As I move to stand in front of the piano (I've heard everyone else walk up to it enough that I can find my way by counting my steps), handing over my binder before I turn my back on the instrument, my mind isn't on the song. Mostly it's scrabbling like a panicked rat in a trap, because I can't follow up Golden Tenor. That's just mean. Why didn't pleasant-sounding laymen like the wannabe princesses gush over him more? They could have eaten up more of my time—all of it for that matter. That would've been great. But the part of my brain that isn't trying to dodge the singing bullet is running over a mental checklist.

Roll your hipbones so the back is not-quite-straight and the pelvic bone is tucked, knees slightly bent, hips level with knees and shoulders, head level; drop the jaw so it hangs there, only moving for letters like "m;" breathe from the diaphragm, keeping the core muscles contracted and ribs out; check the positions of the tongue, throat, palate, chest; exhale as little as possible and allow no air to escape from the nose; ignore the thought that your brain will explode.

I deliver my intro spiel, and nod once that part's over, so that Erik knows I'm ready to start. I can't ruin my setup by speaking to him, and even if I wanted to break that rule of singer/accompanist interaction, my increased heart rate's demanding the bulk of my attention.

The opening chord makes something loosen inside me. And just before I allow what hints of the melody that are provided in the introduction to burst out into the world, I remember Granny saying one of the worst things about the cancer was that she'd have to guess at whose music I would make my own when she was gone.

The lyrics to the song I would have sung at her funeral, had I been brave enough to go, come out hesitant at first, the memory jolting me a little. But I regroup quickly, gather equilibrium, and start to put heart into the phrases.

The melding of rhythm, words, and pitches create a moment where I'm wholly content; the song and the sound are too beautiful for me to feel otherwise. And despite the exertion of my body, the song sounds, and feels, effortless to produce. I feel alive and complete, in a different way than how I would feel singing when Granny was alive, but the sensation is good enough that I don't think I'd mind a recurrence.

When I finish, in the beat of silence that exists between the ending notes and the applause of my peers, I feel as though I'm becoming reacquainted with reality. Somehow, it seems a less hostile place than the one I briefly ascended from during the song.

"Where's that from?" Golden Tenor asks before Professor Harper can begin her critique.

"It's a trunk song. The composer and lyricist just wrote it," I say, oddly breathy, and clear my throat. "It never got put into a story. Oh, and a trunk song is what they'd call songs like that, because they use to just sit around in trunks if people didn't use them in anything."

In other words, the piece was adrift, like me without Granny: the only person in my family who'd understood how good it felt to spill the sounds that lodged in your head, the fragments of stories that suited you in the moment, out into the world.

A pause, then Golden Tenor says abruptly, "Yes."

"You nodded," I guess.

"Uh... yeah. Sorry."

"Yes, how dare you not know how to act around a blind person, having presumably never met one before." This gets a laugh, even from Erik.

"Have you taken lessons before?" Professor Harper asks hopefully, probably only now registering that she'll have to explain things a little differently to me.

"Years ago, but I remember a lot of the technical stuff."

"Do you know what I mean by uh tongue—um—height?"

Shhh. There there, frightened sightie; if I had no clue what you were talking about the worst thing that would happen is that I'd have to touch my own tongue.

I say I do, with enough authority to turn her back into a teacher again, and am able to make some corrections so that the strong muscle almost stays completely wide and unmoving, (my tongue feels sore by the time I'm allowed to go back to my chair and pack up). I coast out the door with the feeling that I'd like nothing more than to curl up in bed for an hour.

But amid the tiredness are surges of adrenaline, a sense of anticipation to see how much more I will have accomplished by this time next week, and there's a smile somewhere inside me that's slowly building up the courage to take shape.

It isn't until I'm back in one of the room's provided metal chairs the following week that I recollect my desire to drop the workshop. But like Miranda said, I would have had to wait for the other classes I'd wanted, and there was every likelihood I'd never get a spot with classes already started.

After some soul scouring, I come to the surprising

conclusion that the logic doesn't make me bristle as much as it did before.

STUDENT TEACHING

by Felix Imonti

CW: Abuse of power

Maria never knew when Captain Howy would be flying into Los Angeles. His visits were always a surprise, so his call at seven o'clock on Friday morning was not unusual. He had flown in the night before from Thailand and was going to take her for a weekend in Santa Barbara. He had already reserved the room. The hotel had a private beach and a closed patio where they could sip rum before going to the king-sized bed where she would show him how much she had missed him.

He didn't ask if she would go. Of course, she would. She was waiting for him. What else would she be doing? It was why he was so generous with her.

This was the first time he was coming from Thailand. Maria wondered what exotic sort of doll he would bring her. He always brought porcelain dolls or glass figurines from wherever he travelled. She set them in a line on a shelf in the living room to remind him of his visits. To be sure that she wouldn't forget to wear them, she put the gold necklace and pearl and diamond ring he had given to her for her birthday on the dresser.

"I will be ready," she told him. Oh yes, and there it was. She heard a tone in his voice that she had heard from other men when they were working up the courage to end a relationship. While she prepared for what was coming, Maria pretended not to understand what was happening. There was a vengeful pleasure teaching the naughty boys that there was a price for playing with dolls.

Her Captain Howy arrived exactly on time in a rented luxury car that cost for the weekend what she was paying for a month rent for her one-bedroom apartment. If he felt so eager to spend money to ease his guilt, she would help him make it a very expensive weekend at the five-star hotel, and dinners at the highest-rated restaurants where she would have lobster and the best champagne.

On Saturday afternoon, they strolled around Santa Barbara so that the fifty-four-year-old balding man could display his twenty-three-year-old trophy. They stopped at a small café for an espresso, and he took her into a jewelry shop where the owner greeted them in an accent that had no national origin. She chatted with her dog about important canine subjects while

Captain Howy purchased a gold bracelet with tiny diamonds for her delicate wrist. After he flew off to one of his other dolls, she would sell the jewelry and the collection of figurines to the shop in Westwood Village where she sold most of her gifts.

Sunday afternoon came slower than she liked. There was the tension of a crisis approaching. How would he end the relationship? Would he do it quietly as if he were regretting what he had to do, or would he need to create a conflict that would allow him to storm out in a prepared rage?

On their way back to Los Angeles, he took side roads and stopped at a couple of wineries. He sampled more wines than she liked before he settled on a case of sparkling wine for her. She was always sure to giggle like a little girl when the bubbles tickled her nose. That would start his slow baritone laugh, watching his little doll being a funny little doll.

She wanted to tell him to stop drinking, but knew better. The usually reserved airline captain would flare. "If I can fly an airplane with two hundred people, I can handle a lousy car."

At the apartment, she ran ahead to open the door. He carried her suitcase in one hand and the case of sparkling wine on his shoulder. The wine was put onto the table and he headed for the still open door.

"I'm double-parked. I better hurry before I get a ticket," and that tight throat sound in his voice was strangling his courage. He was halfway out the door, when he paused. "I won't be able to see you anymore. It was wonderful knowing you." And he was gone. Being always the gentleman, he closed the door quietly.

Thank God, he got it over with without a shouting match. She had been worried she was going to have to end their relationship and wasn't sure how to do it without starting a fight. One way or another, it would have to have ended in two or three months before she began her career as a high school teacher. He was going to be the last of her six lovers that she had known during her years at the university. They had all been generous, married, professional men that liked having a doll waiting for them. They were all sure that they were the only one to play with a blind doll, and who was she to ruin their delusions? Her helplessness made them feel like supermen with her clinging to their arm in small intimate restaurants where others could appreciate how she resembled a doll from *The Magic Toyshop* with huge blue artificial eyes, coal black hair, and a tiny, perfectly proportioned body. She could hear in their voices the pride of men with a human poodle, until they grew bored with the novelty. As far as she saw it, the game was just business to supplement her State Aid to the Blind monthly payment that wasn't enough to feed her guide dog.

She was to begin student teaching in September at a high school where they had already hung out the "unwelcome" sign. With school officials watching and waiting for a reason to break the employment agreement, she would have to be careful about even her private social life. Maybe they would have someone from the school board standing outside of her apartment with a camera to photograph strange men arriving at unusual hours.

Maria was only the third blind university graduate to apply for a teaching position in the public school system. Being a pioneer meant being a target for all of those opposing the change, and she was sure throughout her year as a student teacher that she was being watched at school and around the neighbourhood. During the conferences evaluating her classroom performance, the subject of blindness always entered the discussion. An official asked her, "How will you come to school when it is raining, or what will you do if your dog is sick?" When classes ended in June, she saw their disappointment that she had passed every test. Like it or not, she would return in September a real teacher and knew that they would have unpleasant surprises waiting for her.

A collection of the worst students in the school had been assigned to her compulsory American history class. On the first day, a couple of the rowdies warned her that the principal was watching from the hallway for her class to erupt into bedlam.

"Hey, teach, we're like you. We're no good too," some of them told her.

It was their badge of glory that they displayed a loud bravado in most classes and walked with arms locked together as a wall of defiance along the hallways. At the end of the semester, she hadn't taught them anything, but they had defied the principal by behaving in Maria's class better than they did in their other classes. They celebrated their victory over the system with a cheer that was heard across the campus.

By her third year, the rest of the staff settled on simply ignoring her. And she settled on just teaching. She had the usual mix of students, but there was one who had aroused her curiosity. The others called the student Tom. Tom because he played the bongo drums. When he wasn't tapping out rhythms, he was less than a shadow. Most days, he lingered while she ate lunch in her classroom. He offered to bring her something from the cafeteria or to take out the dog, but she always declined.

She felt a little sorry for the kid without friends. She also worried that his persistence might cause someone to report to the administration what appeared to be questionable behavior by a teacher. When he asked to escort her back to her apartment, she advised him that it would not be a good idea.

Several weeks into the semester, they met accidentally at a supermarket on a Saturday afternoon. She was wearing a backpack and carrying a shoulder bag. He offered to drive her to her apartment. She agreed; it would be better than taking a bus and carrying the heavy bags a couple of long blocks.

"When you have to go shopping, I can drive you," he offered with a worrying enthusiasm.

"I'll think about that," she told him. The prospect of having ready transportation was appealing; the risk of being called to answer for her unusual relations with a male student was a reason to worry. She did mention a couple of weeks later, when he was lingering in the class and no one else was there to hear, that she was going the next day to pick up a new desktop computer. She could not imagine how she was going to be able to carry it up to the second floor.

"I'm not busy tomorrow," he told her, and she decided that saving the taxi fare and the trouble of carrying a heavy machine to her apartment was worth the risk of being called on the carpet.

He was at her door at ten o'clock and they drove thirty minutes to the retailer. On their way back, they stopped for a cup of coffee. While they sipped coffee and nibbled a doughnut, his hand brushed her leg. She ignored it. It might have been an accident. If it hadn't been, then it was better to pretend that it had been.

A couple of weeks later, she mentioned that she would be attending a conference for blind professionals. It was going to be a three-hour ride by bus or a one-hour drive by car and he was willing to wait the four hours that she was expecting to stay. With him being so eager to help, she didn't want to hurt his feelings by refusing.

On the way home, they stopped for coffee and a

piece of New York cheesecake. The tables were small and their knees almost touched. His hand brushed her leg again and she ignored what she knew was a feigned accident.

It was clear and worrying where he wanted to take the relationship. That meant keeping a safe distance. She could never be alone with Tom, but Maria found herself with a problem as the Christmas holidays approached.

Her two female volunteer readers were too busy with family affairs to help her prepare the material for the coming end of the semester. Tom was so eager to spend the day at her apartment helping, he frightened her. Already, other teachers were noticing how much Tom lingered in her class. One of them lived near enough to her apartment to see anyone coming and going. Whispered conferences in the teachers' lounge kept her colleagues up to date about her evenings and weekends.

"Please don't bring your car," she urged him. He understood and came on his bike.

They finished the job in six hours and she ordered a pizza. She opened a bottle of beer, and they munched pizza at her kitchen table. His hand brushed her leg again. This time, it stayed just above her knee under the skirt. She kept sipping her beer and nibbling on the crust of the pizza. She kept nibbling and sipping as the fingers slid along her leg underneath the skirt.

She was wondering how far to go and kept her legs closed tightly. There hadn't been a man since Captain Howy had flown away. Tom was still a little boy and would have to be shown everything.

Maria was teasing herself, playing the coy game as the lovers from her university days must have. How the roles had changed from an innocent, college girl doll with perfectly matched clothes and prepared makeup that the experienced, mature men would have the opportunity to transform into a woman, to a teacher drawing a shy boy into the first levels of manhood. They had been risking their marriages and careers for their dangerous entertainment. She could be gambling her future and throwing away years of hard work just for a little amusement.

"I will make some fresh coffee." She pushed her chair away from the table and his probing hand.

"Don't bother. I have to go." He picked up his jacket and ended the uncomfortable situation.

The time was coming when she would have to decide

about this boy who had been drawn to a blind teacher. Had she become a toy mother for a little boy who did not want to grow up? If it were true or not, would he brag to someone how he was laying a teacher and destroy her future?

Up to that point in their relationship, he wasn't forcing her to set a hard limit. He was satisfied with just being in the same room with her. He always kept their roles of a student and teacher relationship. That was how the semester went and graduation was only days away.

All of the talk on the campus was the big school prom. Tom didn't have a girlfriend and wouldn't be going. During her last year in high school, Maria hadn't been invited to go to the senior prom and listened for the rest of the semester to the other students talking about the exciting night. She didn't say anything to Tom, who she was sure was feeling his isolation.

Two weeks more and the school year was over. About half of the students would be going to various colleges and universities. Tom had been accepted at Cal Poly six hours north of Los Angeles. He would be studying art. His parents gave him a new car for a graduation gift that would enable him to return home on weekends.

On graduation night, 117 students stood in line to receive their diplomas. All of the teachers sat at the rear of the auditorium to watch another class being sent out into the world. Maria knew that Tom would be the forty-third student to march up onto the stage to be given his diploma. Afterwards, he went to his parents to receive their applause. He seemed to have forgotten Maria and she went to her apartment and opened one of the bottles of sparkling wine that was cooling in the refrigerator.

At ten o'clock in the morning, Maria was surprised that Tom was standing at her door. "Would you like a ride in my new car? I can take you shopping as well."

"I'll be right there." Maria didn't care if her snooping colleague was snooping. Tom was no longer her student and no longer of concern to the school board.

"You didn't go to your prom so how will it be if I invited you out for your birthday?" He would be eighteen in one week and an adult. She made reservations at a four-star restaurant across town where no one would know them. At seven o'clock, he arrived in a new suit and in his new car. Even the dog was wearing a blue collar for the evening. As she got into the car, she was wondering if the reporter from the school was watching.

Her date was now old enough to have alcohol. She ordered a white wine and they clicked glasses. When they returned to her apartment, he could have some of Captain Howy's sparkling wine. There were still ten bottles in the case as a testimonial to four years of little life outside of her job.

It was the time for the teacher to teach a boy how to be a man and she moved her classroom to her apartment. "Make yourself comfortable. Take off your tie and jacket," and Maria went to remove her formal clothes. She came back with a loose sweater with buttons up the front and a casual skirt with one snap and five buttons. A bottle was popped open and two large glasses were filled. Half way through the bottle, he found the buttons on her sweater and she instructed him on what nipples were for. He began his education shyly at first and more enthusiastically as the hormones caught the message. She had unfastened his belt and slipped his zipper down. He did hesitate at the snap and buttons on her skirt. She had to take the step for him to give his.

Imagination what only his fingers could know in the

darkened room. When he was at the right level of excitement, the teacher led the student to the bedroom and guided him from boy to man.

Over the summer, she shaped him into a lover that pleased her. Then, he was off to the university six hours away to study art and she was back in the classroom.

On the first day, she heard the rumors about her and a student. The physical education teacher asked her so that the dozen others in the lounge could hear, "Have any interesting little boy students this semester?"

She ignored the jabs. Maria was a professional at ignoring people, but Tom had become more of a problem than the sniping colleagues at the school. During his weekend visits, he was obsessed with marriage. She kept reminding him that he was a student without an income.

"When you have your university diploma, you can have a wife," she assured him after a year of struggling with where her life should go.

Maria had no problem waiting to become the wife of an unknown artist who was going to need time to make his name. Weekend and holiday visits kept her satisfied while she accumulated cash in the bank for the hard years ahead.

Four years went. His parents gave him an aging house for a graduation gift. He had a year to turn it into a studio and to prepare it for his bride.

From the beginning, Maria understood that she would have to continue teaching until the artist was recognized. They were married a year before he sold his first creation. Maria had studied the small statue and could not decide what it was. Even after he explained the meaning of his creation, she could not find anything that inspired an image in her mind.

That was his first and only artistic success. What money he did earn came from odd jobs. He kept assuring her that his oil painting was where he was going to make his name. After wondering for months, she asked about what he was painting. While they sat on the second-hand sofa in the living room, he had her touch the canvas. He described his current masterpiece. He painted in her mind a portrait of a garden scene with a couple of grandparents, a child, and an undefined dog. She saw a tree hanging rich with oranges, flowers in full bloom, and a scene of pure tranquility with soft floating clouds on the horizon.

"I've titled it Paradise," he said with the pride of a

parent naming a child.

He made brush strokes across Maria's imagination, and she asked nothing more about the masterpiece. The artist would need time to have the work recognized.

A year passed. Soon, three years were gone. She was asking herself when the growing number of masterpieces would find a place on a wall in a collector's home or in an art gallery.

On her thirty-sixth birthday, she was wondering what she was getting from her marriage to her boy-husband. He was nine years younger and remained frozen in those fading teenage years when she thought that a child-husband would offer more security than a man who could challenge her. After teaching for ten years, she saw little chance that she could retire to be a mother and housewife. She had to give Tom credit for being a pretty good cook, keeping the house clean, providing her ready transportation, and giving her as much sex as she wanted. All of the services made life more comfortable, but she had outgrown her doubts and needed a real husband. A real husband would have a full-time job, make important decisions, and not always wait quietly for her to decide when it was the time to enjoy her body. The art could be his weekend hobby. Perhaps, in five or ten years, it might become more than an empty promise.

She hadn't bothered mentioning to Tom that she had taken the state examination for a position with the California State Rehabilitation Service. She scored at the top and had accepted a position. It paid more than her teaching job and would end having to deal with the staff that never forgot that she had married a former student who had accomplished little since his graduation. What made the job perfect was that it provided her with a driver to visit clients, a more flexible schedule, and far more independence. She submitted her resignation to the principal and started the job with the State.

The argument with Tom began early on a Saturday afternoon. "You have been screwing me. That means that I am not your mother, so be a real husband and find a job that will allow us to get a decent house and a car that works all of the time."

"I'm an artist," he insisted.

Maria had had someone study the paintings to give her an opinion. "So you keep saying. How long do you think it will take for people to recognize the brilliant artistic talent on those blank canvases?"

221

CATGIRL, HEART AND SKIN

by Melissa Yuan-Innes

CW: Sexual catcalling, misogyny, ableism, internalized ableism, medical emergency

"Give it up for… Catgirl!" The volunteer MC added a little howl.

I drowned him out with the beats for "So What," by Pink, one of Catgirl's favourite songs.

She crawled on the stage. Or at least, I assumed she did, by the barely detectable squeak of her rubber costume rubbing against the wood floor. And from the cheers of the guys at the tip rail. Mostly those guys drank in silence, but everyone loved Catgirl.

I had to imagine her rock moves. I went blind when I was sixteen, so I knew what female anatomy looked like, if only from looking at my own. Nowadays, lots of strippers offered me the goods after hours, hoping I'd spin them the best tunes, which meant I developed moves of my own. But I had to imagine the arch of Catgirl's back or even the delicacy of her toes.

"Take it off!" one of the guys hollered. Then: "Shit!"

She probably lobbed her eye mask into his whisky. Catgirl does not like to be rushed.

I heard her whip smack the ground next. The guys laughed. Mostly they liked to be in charge, but they seemed to find Catgirl amusing.

"C'mere!" yelled another guy.

"Hey, pussy, pussy," slurred a college guy. His buddies laughed, but I rolled my eyes, such as they were. Like we hadn't all heard it ten million times, whether it's Catgirl or any other girl on stage.

Catgirl's whip whizzed through the air and snapped on the edge of the stage.

"Fuck!" the guy yelled, and not in the usual way.

His buddies sniggered.

Most clubs would have canned Catgirl. And a lot of them did. That was how she ended up in El Diablo, at the end of the club strip in London, Ontario, "the insurance capital of Canada." Translation: nowheresville except a university, plus some biker wars spilling over from Detroit.

Whenever Catgirl changed clubs, I followed her.

Old story. I knew that. A hooker with a heart of gold starred in *Pretty Woman*, not reality. But what's reality anymore? Ever since the disease hit, we're all grasping at—whoops, caught myself there. I don't need to find myself clasping reams of plastic tubes. Makes it a lot harder to play the music. And I'm already crippled in one way. I don't need two.

Maybe that's the reason I love Catgirl. Most of us are scared to talk or even think ever since metaphors and similes started coming true. Look what kind of mess I got into, keeping my eyes peeled. I can hardly tell if it's day or night.

Listening to the news is like reading *The National Examiner* in the good old days. At least ten people at the local hospital are whacking buckets with their feet, over and over, praying they'll die, so they can stop kicking. A slew of people in Georgia sleep like infants, which means they nap all the time, day or night, and wake up real crabby. And after one guy came to the club, bragging about his, ah, equine-level equipment, let me tell you, no one has repeated his mistake.

So, most people go to retraining camps. They talk with no embellishment and no surprises.

But Catgirl still dares to fantasize. Right here, right now, at El Diablo.

A man cut into my own fantasy. "You bitch! You little

cunt! You haven't even stripped down yet!"

I amped up the music. I knew Catgirl was still dancing. Pole work now, I bet. Maybe that handstand practically upside down on the bar. She did it once, for me, and let me feel the shape of her body, so I could picture her now levering herself up and almost inverting her body parallel to the pole. I remembered the little gasp she made, lifting herself into the air. I remembered the tremor of her muscles under my hands.

"What the fuck kind of stripper are you, anyway? You think you're the cat's ass? I wouldn't let my German shepherd nail your frigid little twat..."

While Pink sang *na-na-na,* the bouncer dragged away the swearing dude. The other guys razzed him all the way out.

Meanwhile, Catgirl danced. She was an artist, dancing. Not just stripping, although I could always tell when her costume came off from the way the guys howled. She told me she didn't mind showing her breasts, but she didn't always show all the goods, unlike the other girls, who mostly got naked before the second verse and spent most of their time showing off their gash, whether it was through scissoring their legs or, one girl's specialty, licking herself.

Usually, the establishment told the girls what to do and when. One place I knew, you had to give eight lap dances per night, or you owed the suits money. Another one made them sell manicure kits, which was totally bizarre, like it wasn't enough that they sold their bodies for lap dances, they had to hawk forty-dollar nail clippers.

But ever since the disease, the men didn't come out the way they used to. And when Catgirl showed up at El Diablo two weeks ago, they let her write some of her own rules. Even crazy rules, like that she only appeared on stage, she didn't do lap dances, and decided how far to strip. Because when she did get completely naked— and even when she didn't—the club minted.

"Yeah!" a guy growled.

"Hit me baby, hit me…"

"Twenty bucks, sugar, you got it, right here."

I heard Catgirl slide down the pole, her hands squeaking down the metal. The guys got very quiet. I could smell their beer, sweat, and lust.

Thump. I imagined her landing on the stage all fours, giving them the eye, making them wonder if she'd take any of her clothes off at all.

In the microscopic pause between beats, I heard the tiny sound of metal teeth unzipped, followed by a triumphant roar from the guys at the tip rail.

Oh, those breasts. She had hugged me before, so I could imagine them, small and perky and unquestionably real. I pictured her proud brown nipples standing at attention in the meat locker chill of the club. I imagined I was one of the guys at the tip rail, holding out my money, trying to cop a feel, but Catgirl rarely let them touch her.

"She does weird shit," one of the other girls told me yesterday. "She cartwheels up to the rail and steps on the bills and whips 'em into her garter, or she nips the money in her teeth and backs away. Once a guy wanted to stick it down the cheeks of her ass, which the bouncers are supposed to stop, but you know our guys are useless. She let him get real close and then she whipped her ass away from him and snarled like a real cat. He got so scared, he practically shit himself. He didn't give her the money. But she didn't seem to care."

By this point, Catgirl really could have become a cat. The way the disease was going, nothing would surprise me anymore. But I liked to think of her with her perky breasts and her feral attitude, still human.

Another man's voice pierced my thoughts. "Oh, yes, yes, you beautiful little girl..." He was crooning, but respectful, unlike the last guy who got booted. This guy sounded older, maybe in his fifties.

I tensed. Catgirl was my fantasy. I knew that made no sense in a strip club, in a crumbling and decaying world, but that was how I felt. I couldn't bear any serious competition.

"Yes, yes, my darling, my beautiful little cat," he murmured.

I heard Catgirl's footsteps. I imagined her prancing toward him, taking his money, allowing him to stroke her curly black hair or even pinch those little nipples or tug her costume down her hips.

I couldn't bear it.

I cranked up the music. All clubs cut off the music at the three-minute mark, but I was going to drown out that fucker's voice if it was the last thing I did.

I also pumped up the beat, faster and fitter than usual. I knew Catgirl couldn't resist following it, shaking it, slaking it. She never fell behind or off the beat. Don't ask me how I know this when I can't see. A good DJ has almost a supernatural sense of the room. I knew she danced faster and faster still, a whirling dervish of a cat, burning up the stage.

And so I felt it a second before she collapsed.

A millisecond before her body whumped on the floor like a side of beef.

I cut the music.

No one screamed. I think the girls have seen too much to scream.

One of the guys said, "What the fuck?"

The MC said, "Catgirl?" in a confused way, like he expected her to stand up and say "Yes?"

I tripped on the first stage stair, caught myself hard on my hands, and kept running.

"I think something's wrong," said the middle-aged guy I'd been jealous of. "Does anyone know first aid?"

This was all my fucking fault. Why did I have to crank the music?

I skidded to a halt beside Catgirl. Thanks to going blind-o, I'm like a bat with echolocation. Except I twisted my ankle slipping on her tail.

So what. I ignored the pain zipping through my right ankle. I dropped to both knees and felt her face—her closed eyes, imagining the brown skin she'd told me "doesn't melt in your mouth or in your hand," which now felt clammy to touch. I slid my hand over her mouth, over the bump of her jaw, down to her pulse.

No pulse.

Maybe I just couldn't find it. I tracked sideways across her neck, checking for the carotid pulse. I'd felt it in lovers before, idly seeking the reassurance of the bounding pressure against my fingertips, that steady intrinsic rhythm.

Nothing. "Has anyone called 911?" I hollered.

Wait. I was supposed to check her breathing. ABC. Airway-breathing-circulation. I'd screwed up the order. Some DJ I was. I backtracked, tilting her head back— wait. Was I allowed to do that? Could she have broken her neck, falling to the ground? But would I be able to do that frigging jaw thrust?

Fuck it. I put my cheek next to her nose. Nothing. No breathing. You're also supposed to check if the chest rises and falls, so I put my hand between her breasts— no, I did not cop a feel. Her skin was still warm, but that weird moist not-right feel lay on the delicate skin.

Her chest did not rise.

"They're coming. For Chrissakes, they're coming! Get her off the stage!" yelled the manager, but he barely registered in my mind.

I remembered what to do now. I lifted her chin and

tilted her head back. I pressed my lips against hers and blew two breaths in, only vaguely tasting the fake cherry lip gloss and her clove cigarette breath. One long, slow breath. Two.

I felt for her pulse again, quite certain this time, when I located the angle of her jaw and moved south along the column of her neck.

Nothing.

I rolled her flat on her back, flipping her hips so her bum was flat on the stage instead of twisted to the side. Her legs thumped on the ground like dead tree stumps.

No. Not like dead anything.

With renewed fervour, I pressed one hand into her breastbone, laid my other palm on top of my hand, locked my elbows, and started compressing her heart.

I was supposed to count. For some reason, the numbers fifteen and two floated in my mind. But instead of counting, I chanted, "Live. Live. Live. Live."

"I found that fuckin' thing! That automatic thing!" a guy hollered.

I kept compressing. My arms ached already. My breath rasped in my chest. I was goddamn out of shape. But I kept going. Live. Live. Live.

Her chest heaved.

Did I imagine that?

I jerked my chickenst—I mean *skinny*—arms off her chest and fumbled at her throat.

She moaned.

"Get out of the way, you blind bitch!" Someone strong-armed me. I fell on my ass but bounded back up, furious. If anyone knew how to work the AED, it would be me. I took first aid in high school before I'd dropped out.

He thudded the AED on the stage. "Now. Does anyone know how to work this?"

"She's awake, you fuckhead!" I yelled. I lunged at Catgirl's body, trying to feel her breath, her pulse, her anything, but this time she moaned again, louder, and we all heard it.

"She's alive!" said the guy.

"No thanks to you!" I shot back, 'cause the adrenaline still had me torqued up.

And the paramedics finally busted through the door.

As soon as the doctor left, Catgirl rustled the sheets

on her stretcher and said to me, "What are you doing here?"

I licked my lips. They still felt dry. Her heart bleeped along on the monitor at a reassuring, steady rate. I said, "You collapsed on stage."

The nurse's pen stopped scratching on the paper. She was listening to us.

Catgirl said, "I know. I got everything that asshole doctor told me. He thinks my heart is turning into metal."

"That's what he said it looked like on the X-ray." Of course, I had to take his word for it.

"So, I'm turning into the bionic woman, and my heart can't beat right. And he wants to keep me until the morning, so he can wheel me out to his heart doctor friends and tell the world he found a new freak."

That was about the size of it. But I kind of felt too paralyzed to talk to her.

"I knew something was wrong," she said, almost to herself. "I could feel it."

When the doctor had asked her about chest pain and palpitations and shortness of breath, she'd said, "Yeah, yeah, yeah," and wouldn't give any details, probably pissed off that they all kept laughing about how she'd collapsed during a pole dance. And of course, they couldn't get over her costume. "It even has a tail!" one of the nurses said.

Catgirl cracked her knuckles. "I know you," she said to me now. "DJ Fresh." Her voice echoed in the room. In the distance, I heard an ambulance's siren advancing on the hospital.

She said, "You've been following me around."

I considered playing it cool. But I'm blind, and she almost died, so what's the point? I said, "Yes."

"You're in love with me," she said.

I shrugged. I knew she could see the movement, even though I hated when other people shrugged because I had to guess from the silence and the rustle of their clothing.

She said, "I don't do girls."

Even though I'd been braced for that, it still felt like a knee in the solar plexus. I hunched a little like I could protect myself after the fact. Tears sprang to my eyes. I blinked them away. Rejection is nothing new for a queer girl, although I have to admit, I corner the market on self-destruction: falling in love with a stripper is a dead end, even before her heart literally turns to gold.

Catgirl waited a beat. "And I don't do kids. How old are you, anyway?"

I shrugged again.

"Seriously," she said.

"Seventeen," I admitted. "But I've got really good fake ID."

"Huh. I'm twenty-five. I'm old enough to be your math tutor."

I had to laugh. It sounded rusty, but she always managed to surprise me. I said, "Diablo Cody."

"Huh?"

"That's where you got that line, right? Diablo Cody. Her stripper memoir, *Candy Girl*. You read it?"

"Yeah. A long time ago. Ouch." She raised her voice above the sound of a motor rumbling beside the bed. "Nurse. This thing hurts my arm."

The nurse bustled beside us. "It's just your blood pressure cuff. Keep your arm straight, Catherine."

"The name's Catgirl. And it hurts."

"It'll be over in a minute."

Catgirl swore under her breath. The motor stopped and a ticking began. The nurse said, "Good. 110/70. Very nice, ah, Catgirl."

"I'm leaving," said Catgirl.

"Oh, no. I'm going to get Dr. Lanofsky—"

"You do that. I'm not a science experiment." I heard the sound of Velcro ripping. "DJ. Help me get this friggin' bedrail."

I slid my hands along both the cool metal rail, searching for a lever.

"Up near my head. The red thing. Here!" She guided my arm, and I pulled up on a lever. The bedrail fell.

"I'm calling security." The nurse scurried back to the phone.

"Call away," said Catgirl.

"You're leaving against medical advice. You'll have to sign a form—"

"You know what you can do with that form."

"You can't use a lighter in here!" Panic tightened the nurse's voice.

I heard the lighter scritch. I smelled smoke and burning plastic. I caught my breath, but Catgirl said, "No worries, DJ, I'm just burning off my IV. Now. Let's kick it."

She grabbed my hand, vaulted off the bed, and started running. I raced beside her, even though I had no idea where we were going or if we would make it. But I ran away with Catgirl's slim little hand in mine.

LIFE AFTER DARK

by Anita Haas

CW: Internalized and external ableism, mention of misogyny, violence

Tom's head felt like an egg cracking in an oven. Afternoon sun sliced through his clenched eyelids, as he groped around in panic. Where was his visor, his windbreaker, his sunglasses? Where were Laura and Ben?

He pushed himself up, patting the area around him—rock, sand, twigs. He allowed one eye to open a sliver for a split second, like when doctors forced drops into them. The image imprinted itself on his retina, and he waited the seconds for it to fade so he could have an idea of his surroundings. *Like those old darkrooms where photographers used to watch their film develop, little by little, in tubs full of chemicals,* he remembered explaining to someone once. *I watch the image slowly appear after I shut my eyes and the light fades.* But all the washed-out images told him was that he was stranded.

The terrain was too uneven for him to walk without

tripping. A challenge, even with dark lenses.

Laura had suggested a picnic. Something which didn't entice Tom. "It's not like we're city people who have to drive for hours to see a tree." But she had insisted. Ben was coming too. That set alarm bells ringing in Tom's head, but what argument did he have? And after lunch and several beers, they had all dozed off, him with his windbreaker covering his face.

He had been the victim of pranks before. Versions of *blind man's bluff,* and *pin the tail on the donkey*, the purpose being to witness him stumble, grope, and blunder. *Innocent fun*, he told himself, *nothing to get riled about*. He would just have to wait until they got bored of their game.

But after an eternity of about five minutes, rage bested his better judgment. "Okay, you bastards! Show's over!" This time they had gone too far.

Giggles, snapping branches, the slam of pickup truck doors, and the grumble of a motor told him they would not let him have the last word. They were leaving.

He turned to his right and blinked his eyes open, remembering the shade tree there, then waited for the blaze to fade in his eyes before he could see the image and blinked again. *Like a slide show of photographs*. As long as the objects around him stayed put, he was okay. It was moving objects that were difficult, because by the time the fading image told him something was approaching, it would have already hit him, or if a familiar face was coming his way, it would have passed him by, ungreeted.

Now that Ben and Laura were gone, he didn't care if he made a spectacle of himself as he crawled over mud and rock, twigs digging into his palms, toward the tree.

The leaves and branches soothed his wrath with their shade. He would wait for the sun to drop behind the far horizon and sheathe its sabre for the night, then slide his feet cautiously over the ground, arms held out for balance, until he reached the road's flat surface, and walk home.

"I never understood why you left Somerleigh..." Laura hesitated, "well, Canada."

Seven years had passed. Tom was living in Madrid. Laura had married Ben shortly after Tom left

Somerleigh, and she had two kids before divorcing. Tom had seen Laura the previous Christmas while visiting his parents, and she hadn't stopped emailing and WhatsApp-ing him since. She had even invited herself to visit this Christmas.

"Oh, lots of reasons," Tom began. "Even as a little kid, when *Babcia*, my grandmother, told me about the old days and read me stories from books about Poland, I knew Europe was the right place for me."

They were coming out of the Atocha train station, and strolling towards Lavapiés, the part of old Madrid where Tom lived. That evening, they were invited to the Almudena Cathedral, where Silvia, a colleague of his, was giving a Christmas concert with her choir. All the teachers were going.

He loved this time of year in the city. It was invigorating. It got dark early, and the lights illuminated the glorious buildings, all within eye's reach.

"Well, it's pretty, sure," Laura admitted as they passed the Reina Sofía Museum. "All the history and art and everything. But to live… I guess it's just a matter of taste. I prefer the country. Wide open spaces."

"That's just the point. To live! For me, it was both taste and necessity."

"Well, you do seem happier, more confident. Has your vision improved?"

"Not at all. I have achromatopsia: no colour vision, day blindness, and extremely poor visual acuity. Work is still a challenge, but this city is accessible. I feel more independent here than in Somerleigh."

Tom's family had settled in the sleepy university town of Somerleigh, Ontario. His early years were spent in *Babcia's* apartment downtown, where she babysat him and his older brother, Mathew, while his father worked as a mechanic and his mother cleaned houses, her English not good enough to continue teaching kindergarten.

Everything in *Babcia's* books about Europe enthralled him. Cities were compact, buildings snug together. Not like Somerleigh. Even as a child, he perceived how distances in Canada seemed to stretch. And when he got close enough to see things, they were not like *Babcia's* books. Europe for him meant picturesque gardens, statues, pavilions, stone pathways, ornate lampposts, and footbridges over streams full of ducks. All with backdrops of castles, stone walls and wrought iron gates.

"How is Madrid more accessible?"

They were waiting at a busy traffic light on the Ronda de Atocha. "Do you hear that beeping?"

"Uh, yes."

"That is the traffic light letting me know I can cross. But I would know, anyway, because there are so many people on foot here, all crossing together."

"We have traffic lights in Somerleigh, too, wise guy."

"Oh? On Harper Road, or a dozen others like it. Have you ever crossed them?"

"No, but..."

"There is half a kilometre between traffic lights."

"Good exercise!" Laura giggled.

"Yeah, like in the winter when you have to navigate long stretches of glaring snowdrifts before you can cross the road, and then walk all the way back on the other side to get to where need to go, and you are running late for a class or a job interview… because I suppose you never noticed from your car window that there are no sidewalks there." Tom could feel the old angry monster rise inside him. He was cagey about sharing his experiences with others, but if Laura wanted to pick up from where they had left off years before, there were some things she would need to know.

Laura shrugged. "But everybody drives…" She stopped herself.

He reminded her of how many Somerleigh buildings lay far from the road, beyond expanses of parking lots, their signs and numbers too far away to see. "And you need to drive for everything! Here, if I want to get my hair cut, I've got a dozen choices within a five-minute walk. Same if I want to buy groceries, or see a play, go to the gym, to a museum, take a dance class, or learn Greek! And if I can't find what I want in this neighbourhood, there is the subway"—he pointed to it as they passed—"the train station we just came from, or a dozen buses. And Lavapiés is so international, you can find shops and restaurants specializing in cuisine from India, China, Morocco, you name it!"

"Yes, but where does everybody park?" She frowned.

Eye doctors had handed his parents a fistful of medical terms and sent them on their way. Bewildered and intimidated, they had thanked him, shrugged, and accepted their plight. Frustrated, they didn't know how or if they should help their son.

They bought a small farm, confident it was the best thing for their children. *Normal* children chased balls in the sunshine. *Good* children went to bed before dark. Tom seemed to hate everything normal and good. He felt more isolated than ever. He could no longer walk to the library with *Babcia,* or to her Polish butchers and bakers. There were no buildings with interesting lines and shapes to gawk up at in the early evening light. And, if sidewalks were sparse in town, their surfaces bumpy and unpredictable, there were absolutely none in the country, his knees eternally scraped from tripping.

"Oh, the country! You will love it." cooed a friend of *Babcia's*, "All those beautiful colours! The birds and flowers, the changing fall leaves and the sunsets!" Of course, he could see none of those things, but the magical morning bird-choirs delighted him.

He missed the evenings in town, where streetlamps guided him, gently picking out objects normally lost in the glaring wash of day: a bench of gnarled, knotted wood; a willow, weeping in a corner yard; or the arched brows of a creaky, grandfatherly house smiling down at him.

"I've got my boy, Matt, to help with the outdoor chores," he overheard his father quip to a neighbour once, "and Mama has her *girl*, Tom, to help in the house."

Mama sighed whenever Tom had dusted badly. She wondered if he really could not see or if he had been making excuses to get out of helping. The boys at school excluded him from their games and the girls coddled him like one of their dolls. He spent recess pressed flat against the brick school building, not daring to step forward so wayward balls and screeching children wouldn't collide into him.

So, the school library had become his oasis. He felt marvellously at home in the subdued light, the hush. Volunteering there permitted him to spend recess indoors. He learned the Dewey decimal system and shelved the three-tiered cart well before the dreaded buzzer wailed. He treasured the precious remaining minutes curled up behind a study carrel in the far corner, a book pushed up against his face, drowning in the worlds he was discovering in all those pages. Worlds where balls, colours, cars, and sunlight didn't matter.

Tom's teachers had been told he should sit in the front row. Job done. The truth was that Tom could have been sent to sit in the last row—it made no difference; he could not see the board from the front row, either. To see the sentences, he would have had to walk back and forth directly in front of the board, then climb a chair or bend down to read the writing above or below eye level. But that way, he would not only be blocking the board for others, but also call embarrassing attention to himself and using his eyes as an excuse. Besides, the teachers had been so proud of how well they were handling this "challenged" child, that he hated to disappoint them. He developed great memory skills, and was encouraged to borrow other pupils' notebooks if necessary. That added to his unpopularity.

"I forgot my gym shorts." Tom stood, wincing in front of his teacher one day.

Tom never forgot anything. Especially not the

nightmare of gym class. He hated to lie but if there was anything worse than recess outside, it was gym. The two things most kids loved. He lay awake at night, his stomach in knots, remembering the humiliation of being the last one chosen for a team, then having to worry about being hit by the unseen flying object. Gym class consisted of volleyball, basketball, baseball, dodgeball, soccer, or hockey. No matter what the curriculum said. What about gymnastics, wrestling, judo?

"Again?" the teacher frowned and gave him the detention Tom preferred. He could stay behind and read!

"Why didn't you say anything?" Laura demanded. "I'm sure the teachers would have understood! There are thousands of disabled kids out there." They had stopped for a *caña con limón* in one of the traditional bars in Tirso de Molina Square.

"That's just it. I was never considered disabled."

"But you are legally blind, right?"

"Officially, yes. But we didn't know that then, and I certainly never think of myself as legally blind. In fact, I still think I see *normally*, until I notice that what I have to hold up to my face, others can see from practically across the room! But, think about it, Laura, do I look disabled to you?"

She looked down at her glass. "Honestly, no."

"A nurse once accused me of lying when I said I couldn't read the chart beyond the second row. She told a waiting room full of people that I would not have been able to walk there unassisted if it were true. So embarrassing! You see, I don't walk into walls, and I don't fall down stairs, but it seems I have to do that for some people to believe I can't see the board, or that menu over there, or distinguish between the different foods in a buffet."

"Really?"

His inner monster was stirring again. He had learned to tame it over the years, but sharing these memories with Laura was like poking at a campfire. "Sorry. I hate whining, but if a medical professional doesn't believe an adult, would a teacher believe an eight-year-old?"

"Hey, you, kid!"

Young Tom could see a group crossing over the street towards him. Some taller, others shorter. He could usually distinguish between boys or girls, but no faces. He recognized them by their voices, if he knew them.

"What colour is this?" the tall kid shouted, pulling at his jacket.

Tom would guess, "Blue?" Shrieks and giggles from the kid's audience told him it was not blue. Other times, he would just say he didn't know.

Sometimes the fun stopped there, other times it got nasty.

"I never understood why," Tom said. "If I was famous to a bunch of kids I didn't even know, precisely for not seeing colour, why did they keep asking me? Did they spend their free time giggling at TVs that didn't work?" He and Laura were laughing now.

The crowds were thickening as they approached the Puerta del Sol. "This area is crazy this time of year," he shouted over the din, and smiled. "Then one day, when I was fourteen, a pretty girl named Laura sat next to me on the school bus."

She smiled. "That sure got Ben jealous!"

And a rivalry sprung up between Ben and Tom, which would last for years.

Tom's free time during his teen years was spent in the barn, with the sweet scent of hay and slivers of light filtering through cracks in the roof, like stars at night. But the best part was the cats. Elegant and cautious, they sniffed out their surroundings before proceeding, alert for danger, just like him.

Here, he set up weights and a punching bag, compensating for his lack of ball-chasing, and car-driving skills by building muscles. He signed up for judo and joined the school wrestling team.

"Don't you miss home?" They had passed the masses of revellers in the city's largest square and were now being pushed along by the crowds past the many shops on Calle Arenal towards the opera house.

"Some things, sure." It was still noisy, but they no longer needed to shout.

"You live in an old, one-room apartment here. If you came back, we… you could live in a big, new house."

"The prison of suburbia!" Tom shuddered.

She looked confused at first, then protested, "I would drive you everywhere. I used to pick you up when we went on dates."

"You say that now, Laura. But soon, I would become a burden. You'd resent having to be my chauffeur, my taxi driver. Here, I don't need anyone to drive me. Public transport is excellent. There are sidewalks everywhere. I don't have to ask for favours I can't return, always feeling indebted."

Public transportation in Somerleigh was limited to a few scant bus routes connecting the university to downtown. "Waste of taxpayers' money," his father always grumbled. "Who needs buses? Everybody drives!" Fortunately, home had only been an hour's walk from town.

"But the subway is colour-coded," Laura pointed out. The trip from the airport to the city centre had been uncomfortable and confusing for her.

"And number-coded!"

"Wow, I wouldn't be able to remember all those numbers!"

"No? Are you number-blind?" Tom could hear his voice sharpen. "There are only twelve. I have memorized all the numbers and the colour names." They had arrived at Isabel II Square in front of the opera house. He expected to see Laura's jaw drop in awe at the sight of the building which never failed to amaze him, but she barely gave it a glance.

She looked sheepish. "We could move to Toronto. There is a subway and lots of immigrants you could teach English to."

At the strike of sixteen, every good citizen of Somerleigh became a car driver, if not owner. Parents smiled proudly and younger siblings looked on with admiration, awaiting their turn. The car was a rite of passage. It gave one status, independence, power, and showed the world how hard you worked. Tom was often forced to give explanations as to why he didn't drive but was met with looks of suspicion.

"I think you are exaggerating. People like to help," Laura insisted.

They had circled around the opera house, and were heading toward the ornate Sabatini Gardens. Tom hoped they would make more of an impression on her.

"I don't mind doing someone a favour now and then," she added.

"It's like banks." Tom explained, "If you are rich, they are always willing to lend you more money. If you are poor, no one will lend you a dime. The same with favours. If you really need one, it becomes a bargaining tool. People say things like, *'What's in it for me?,'* *'That's ten minutes out of my way!'* Or… *'Any time! But I can't today. And tomorrow I'm busy. Maybe next week, or the week after.'* My brother, Matt, used to play power games by purposely showing up half an hour early or an hour late. If I complained, he would holler, 'Hey man, I'm doing you a favour, remember?'"

Tom didn't remind Laura of the high school dance they had attended together years before. All the other guys had driven up with their dates in the passenger seat. He had overheard Laura joke to some friends, "In this relationship, *I'm* in the driver's seat."

Tom's brother had become a mechanic, like his father. The family discouraged Tom from applying to university.

"You just stay here on the farm and let me take care of you," his mother urged him. She seemed to enjoy her identity as Poor Annie, the invalid boy's mother.

But Tom decided to attend Somerleigh College and stay with *Babcia* during the week. He chose English literature, which made his father grunt and leave the room when he told him.

At university, he discovered a new world. It was challenging; he still couldn't see the board or screens, and he studied into the wee hours, eyes and neck aching, but fortunately, most classes were lectures. Here, people talked about things other than parking and gas prices. He practiced the new skills he'd learned in language classes on foreign friends, their accents evoking exotic places. He delighted in learning about their music, history, cuisine, and literature. He enjoyed the freedom of anonymity here, and social activities mostly took place in the evenings when he could disguise his vision problem best.

He used all his coping strategies. When asked if he squinted because he was tired or sick, he would say yes. If he lost his way, he would knock his forehead with the heel of his hand and say, "How clueless of me!" If people asked why he wore dark glasses indoors, he joked that he was a movie star incognito. If he was meeting someone, he would arrive early, so they would have to look for him and not the other way around. He avoided eye contact, so if he didn't say hello, people would not take him for a snob. It seemed more credible to be forgetful, slow, lazy, clumsy, or just odd, than visually impaired.

But Tom needed money, like everyone else. Barring outdoor jobs, and ones that required driving, colours, or visual acuity, finding work was still not easy.

"I remember you had lots of odd jobs," said Laura.

They were in the lovely gardens beside the royal palace. The air was crisp and smelled of trees. Streetlamps lit their way along the paths in the dusk, and they were able to speak without having to shout, as they had left the shopping multitudes behind.

"I worked for about a week in the campus bar, but since I couldn't see the menu on the wall, I had to memorize it. The problem was they had to change it constantly, and that led to some embarrassing screw-ups! Added to that, I couldn't see the customers waving to get my attention. I remember my manager said I looked half asleep, you know, the squinting. He asked me if I smoked a lot of dope!"

"The nerve!" Laura rolled her eyes.

Tom laughed, "Yeah, and then my buddy, Roger, offered me a pizza delivery job. I told him, 'Sure! I could carry the pizza to its destination, assuming there is a sidewalk!'"

"Didn't you work in the library once?" Laura seemed to relax in the calm of the gardens.

"Oh, yeah!" Tom shook his head and collapsed on a bench, "What a disaster that was!"

Lizzie, a classmate, worked in the university library and encouraged Tom to apply.

"But, you know, I don't see that well. Would they hire me?"

"You see fine! Go on. Try!"

"We are equal opportunity!" chirped the head librarian during the interview. "In fact, Arthur over there works at his desk from a wheelchair. And he is much more disabled than you are."

There were the three-tiered carts he remembered from volunteering. He was grateful to be back in the hush of a library, to breathe in the fragrance of paper and to disappear among the stacks. The books that lived at eye level were the easiest to locate. For higher shelves, he would climb up on the footstool, and to see the tiny decimals on the highest shelves, he would pull books down and hold their spines to his face, often dislodging and returning several before finding the correct place. He crouched down for the lower shelves and lay almost flat on the floor for the bottom ones. Soon, the cart was empty, and he wheeled it to Marge, his manager, at the book station.

"Is that your first cart?"

His face grew hot. "Yes."

"Lizzie's just shelved four. And Brian here is finishing his fifth."

Mortified, Tom saw Brian insert his last books. He took one, and with barely a glance, reached up and slipped it between its neighbors, then grabbed the next, and swung it down to a lower shelf.

"You have to work faster," he could hear Marge scolding.

"Well, I don't know if they mentioned it, but I can't see very well."

She looked at him doubtfully, and he knew what she was thinking. Here was a perfectly strong, healthy-looking young man who didn't bash into walls or trip over things, and he was using his vision as an excuse for being slow!

"Just work faster."

He nodded. Maybe he didn't have to be *so* exact. If the book was a little further up or down the shelf, who would know? This time there was no lying on the floor, no pulling books off top shelves.

Marge frowned. "A little better. Lizzie shelved three carts and Brian four. Tom, you are just too slow."

Tom hated that word. It made him sound like he wasn't capable of understanding the task, or as if he were goofing off instead of working.

Marge shook her head, "Maybe the head librarian has something else you can do."

Tom recognized that wash-my-hands-of-you tone, but decided to see the boss, just in case.

"No. A lot of what we have here is colour-coded. You wouldn't be able to do that." The head librarian told him when he consulted her.

"And the checkout?" Tom's voice sounded desperate.

She shook her head, "Our patrons would feel uncomfortable watching you peer at the computer screen."

But what about all that equal opportunity stuff? He wished he could ask.

She seemed to read his mind. "Oh! We love people

with disabilities. Look at Arthur!"

"Of course, I couldn't expect them to *uncolour*-code things just for me, or to pay me the same as others when I took four times longer!" Tom said.

"Hmm. I suppose not." Laura had taken a seat next to him.

"And then she said," Tom raised his voice, imitating the librarian, "'there are lots of jobs you can do. Just not here! Thousands of blind and deaf people work. People without arms or legs!'"

"Yes!" Laura jumped in, excited, "I heard about this blind concert pianist, and there's this Olympic champion with no legs and..."

Tom let her ramble on. He had heard all about those concert pianists, Olympic champions, and rocket scientists. As if being disabled gave you some secret formula for excellence. And since he was not *as* disabled as most of them, he was expected to have achieved all those things and more! But how? How could a blind woman be a concert pianist if she couldn't see the sheet music? When he screwed up in music class because he couldn't see the notes, he just got yelled at. And it was interesting to note that all the people who insinuated he should be all these things and more, were themselves not concert pianists, Olympic champions, or rocket scientists, either.

"And really, Tom," Laura's voice sounded like a mother scolding her son, "you really are lucky you are not blind."

"Absolutely!" he responded to yet another senseless comment he had heard a million times, then surprised the satisfied look off her face, by adding, "And so are you!"

Eventually Tom found a job tutoring Somerleigh high school students in English and French. He volunteered as an English teacher to new immigrants, and loved it. He yearned to visit all the places they came from, taste their food, tap his toes to their music, and learn their lingo.

"So, that is what made you decide to become an ESL teacher?" They had reached the lovely square in front of the palace and were enjoying a glass of rosé wine in the pricey but elegant Café del Oriente. "How are we for time, by the way?"

"Fine," said Tom. "The concert's at nine. We still have forty minutes. Well, you see. I realized I had to find a job where I would be paid for the finished product, so the only person who would suffer from my *slowness* was me."

"Oh, like getting paid per book shelved, instead of per hour of shelving?"

Tom was impressed. "Exactly! They wouldn't have complained then, would they? It takes me ages longer than other teachers to prepare, grade, and so on, but they pay me for the hour of class, not my preparation hours."

"Oh, but that is unfair to you, isn't it?"

"Maybe. I don't know. Everyone has their problems. This one is mine."

"And why Spain, exactly?"

"My buddy, Roger, suggested we go to Europe together after graduation." He chuckled, "He was always falling in love with exchange students. Had a different girlfriend every week! So, his post-graduation destination kept changing, too!"

"What a guy! So, he had a Spanish girlfriend?"

"Yes, well, for a while anyway. Can you believe it? I am here, and not in France or Germany or Italy, because of Roger's love of the month!"

He'd had a lot of time to think that day, seven years before, while he waited for the forgiving dusk, and even more time on the angry twenty minute hike home. Ben and Laura had mercifully left his jacket, phone, and glasses just beyond reach of his day vision.

Tom finally reached his parents' farmhouse. He could see much better now, in the low light. Ben was smoking by his pickup. "Hey, man! We thought something happened. Did you get lost? *Hahaha!*"

"Tom!" Laura rushed towards him. "Are you okay?"

Something had happened. No, he was not okay.

"Hey, man. Don't get sore." Ben started at Tom's expression. "It was only a joke!"

Ignoring both Laura and his family, Tom strode towards Ben, grabbed the front of his T-shirt with his left hand and bashed his face with his right.

That's for who you are and what you did.

Ben, astounded, was slow to react.

Then Tom whacked with his left. *That's for every brat who taunted me in the schoolyard.*

Right. *For all the fuckers who think if you don't drive a car at sixteen you are lazy.*

Left. *And this one is for the bitch in the library.*

Right. *For the teachers who made me go to gym class.*

Left. *That one is for Dad calling me a girl.*

Right. *For the bastard who wouldn't let me rent a DVD because I didn't have a drivers' license. Fucker didn't even know what a passport was!*

Left. *For all the girls who didn't want to dance with me, and… a knee in the nuts for the girl you took away from me!*

Punch, punch, punch. They were on the ground now. A demon had sprung to life inside Tom, and Ben was feeling the fruits of all those years of weightlifting and bag-punching.

Ben represented everything he hated about this place. Nothing more than a hillbilly, whom everyone in this hick-town thought was God Himself.

"Tom! Stop!" Laura screamed.

As his rage spent itself, Tom realized Ben was no longer fighting back. He heard shrieks. Hands grabbed his shoulders, and he allowed Mathew to pull him off. He saw the bleeding mess he had made of Ben. He flung his brother's hands off and marched past his mother toward the house.

This was it. He knew. But that was okay. They could all go straight to hell. He wanted nothing more to do with this place.

"Poor Ben," he said now as they were finishing their second glass of rosé.

"No. You did right. Ben's a bastard." They got to their feet and headed toward the dazzling façade of the palace.

He looked over at her. "You didn't think that way at

the time. You stopped speaking to me until last Christmas!"

Laura bowed her head. "We were shocked. You were always so easygoing. Never got mad about anything..."

"Oh, yes I did! Just knew how to keep it all in, that's all. Until that day."

"Well, so, is everything perfect here, then?"

Tom paused. Should he tell her about all his daily trials and tribulations? About how just last week, he had lost a job opportunity because, after carefully locating the site of the interview a few evenings before—as he always did when he had to go somewhere new—there was a last-minute change? The interview would be in a place he had not staked out in advance. He got on the wrong bus, arrived an hour late, stressed and frazzled, and the interviewer refused to see him.

"Well, I still can't see most street signs or bus numbers. Almost missed a plane at Heathrow once because I got on the wrong-coloured inter-terminal bus. No, still can't see the board, but since I'm the teacher now, I know what's on it because I put it there!" He laughed. "And since I can't see the PowerPoints on screens, I hope to God my students don't put porn pictures in their presentations! Or cheat during exams!

Come on, the cathedral is this way."

"What?" She giggled. "And what do your bosses say?"

"Say to what? They are paying for the finished product, remember? How I get it done is my business."

"But... isn't it a bit dishonest?"

"So, you think I should walk into a job interview and say, 'Pleased to meet you. Just so you know, I can't see the board, or the screen, or the computer monitor, or the textbook, or the students' faces beyond the second row... and by the way, I almost got lost coming here.'?"

"I... I don't know."

"Right. Neither do I. But I do know that I have rent to pay just like everybody else. And the last thing I want is to end up back on the farm, and be Mama's poor invalid boy again."

"Oh, Tom!" Laura sounded distressed. "I could help you. Come back with me. We can move to a big city. There are self-driving cars now. You would finally fit in, be like everyone else!"

Tom thought of all the trials he lived through every day. Would those be easier in Toronto? How he used to long to fit in! To be like everyone else, be accepted by his family, his classmates, Laura. And how faraway that all seemed now, in this city, which had adopted him and which he now called home. He was going through culture shock just being with Laura now.

"No, Laura. You belong there. I belong here."

"Loads of experiments are being done. I heard there are tests... you may even be able to see colour one day!"

"Seeing colour has never been that important to me. I spend my days looking down, hiding from the sun and watching where to place my feet. Then, at night, the city changes. I look up, up at the winking stars, the soothing velvet sky. The illuminated buildings smile down at me."

They had arrived at the glowing cathedral and strolled to the far side of the square overlooking the escarpment. Tom smiled up at the stunning palace to his right, then at the columns of the looming cathedral to his left. He wondered what it would be like to see all the details instead of just smudges.

"Laura, if the world were any more beautiful than this, I don't think I could stand it."

INSPIRATION PORN STAR

by M. Leona Godin

CW: Internalized ableism, mentions of suicidal ideation, mention of fatphobia, racism

Fifteen years ago, before the fame, the fortune, and this backstage-bathroom cringing all began, I got paired with my first guide dog. My friends expected I'd make Magnum (when you go to guide dog school, you don't get to name your dog) take me to the bar STAT, but what surprised everyone (including me) was how I began checking out the open-mic comedy scene of the Lower East Side. Although I'd always hated jokes—at least the kind Dad (may he rest in peace) used to torture us kids with of the "an Irish, a Jew, and a Chinese walked into a bar" variety—I thought I might try my hand at stand-up.

Not being able to see is just kind of naturally funny. Lots of laughs dealing with people who think you're an alien from Planet Blind and the constant slapstick of bumping into stuff. Life as a pinball is hilarious if you look at it the right way.

I maybe pre-empted the guide dog thing a tad bit, but whatever. It was after an ugly breakup, and how could I find a new boyfriend if I couldn't get to the bar? I could still see some, sure, but at night, my vision sucked. I needed my freedom, and I wasn't about to start wagging a white cane around New York City.

Those early open mics were part exhilarating, part humiliating. The thousands of performances have run together over the years for sure, but I'll never forget the first time Magnum and I stepped onto the little raised stage into the spotlight. I was emphatically not blind back then. I was visually impaired and pretty sensitive to bright lights. But I stared down the spot and earnestly delivered my not-too-funny monologue, which included some quasi-jokes about whacking people on the streets as I trotted past with Magnum's harness handle in my left hand and my cellphone in my right, elbow sticking out. The punchline was something like, "Beware of blind girls bearing cellphones."

That was back when cellphones were actually used as phones, before they started talking with electronic voices that made them accessible. Of course, back then, they were just phones with little tactile keypads.

No problem. Until people started texting. My sighted friends—actually, all my friends are sighted—texted me and for like a year none of them realized I wasn't texting back.

Don't get me wrong, I'm not looking for blind friends. One blind person in a room is a novelty, two's discomforting, and three or more's a circus. Not the fun kind.

Anyway, one day my boyfriend at the time was fiddling with my phone. He said, "Did you know there were all these texts in here?"

"Um, no," I said. "How would I know that? Who're they from?

"Like everyone. Oh, here's one from me."

All that's different now. I can text like a champ with my talking smart phone with GPS that tells me where to go, and it reads books and all sorts of things that were really hard before. So, I'm not ashamed to say it: I love the electronic voice that chatters in my earbud constantly. Her factory name is Daniella. She's got personality.

I didn't get a whole lot of laughs from my early "comedic" monologues, but people were confused and intrigued. Fellow comedians encouraged me to keep going. I think they didn't feel much competition with my act. I mean, I cornered the market on sex and blindness jokes, so they didn't have to worry about me eating into their dick-joke territory.

Occasionally one of them would be inspired by my act to try their hand at a Helen Keller type joke, but it usually just made everyone feel uncomfortable and died, and I learned to just smile like a Cheshire cat and let it wash over me.

I started wearing sunglasses to help with the glare and fake eye contact. These were not clunky black wrap-around blind man glasses, but super cool and sexy silver steampunk shades that I used to my advantage.

I incorporated this bit into my act where I'd say, "Yes, I do have superpowers. Like, I can see all of you right now—right through your clothes. You're all naked." Then I'd turn my head to the first little sigh or nervous titter. Another would inevitably follow, and another. Each time I turned my head to the voice until there were too many to point at with my "stare that sees right through you" (as one notable reviewer would later put it). It didn't always blow up into full laughter, but at least one person after my set would come up and say—sometimes with real anger—"You're not blind!"

Eventually, I had a genuinely funny routine, including that gem that they would use in the vodka bubbly spiked seltzer commercial I was in years later: "I don't feel like a blind person when I'm having sex. Unless I get mixed up with some freak. Some freaky-freak with a fetish for eye contact."

I got to be a regular at this comedy showcase down on Ludlow that was popular. It was definitely not one of those pricey clubs in Midtown, but it was lively and crowded, and attracted folks in the biz. One night after my set, a male voice—part slick and smarmy, part serious and capable—said in my ear, "That was great. Do you have representation?"

Magnum and I stepped one step away from the voice and I said, "Representation?"

"Do you have an agent?"

"No," I said, pulling a smoke out of my pocket, preparing to head outside.

"Here's my card," he said, flapping it under my fingers that were holding the cigarette, since my other hand was holding onto Magnum's harness. I ignored it.

"I can't read that, douchebag," I said, making him feel small. "Give it to one of your own kind."

That's when one of my buddies, Mike (who had apparently been hovering), swooped in and said, "The man's legit. Don't be dumb, Maryann, give him your damn number."

"My name's Dan," said the agent. "Can I buy you a beer?"

"Jameson on the rocks," I said. And he buggered off to buy it.

I get nicer with a little booze in me, so we kept talking.

"I'm Lola's agent," he said. "You know her?"

"That lesbian Filipina who tells jokes about knives and vaginas and being the only female line cook in a four-star restaurant?" I said. "Sure, just heard her Comedy Central half-hour special."

I was hooked. Dan had a predilection for offbeat

talent, and so my "somewhat slutty, almost always drunken, angry blind chick schtick" was solidly in his wheelhouse. He found me a manager, Bill, and helped me move into headliner spots and then tours around the country. Nothing I'd known before had felt better than stand-up: small chuckles and titters swelling into full-body laughter that rolled up the rows of audience to swirl onstage with me like a blankie made entirely of love and admiration.

When Ron—Ronald Price, the heartthrob Marvel movie sidekick—came to one of my shows, we fell in love at first sight/first feel, respectively. I was making good money by then, and Ron was generous in the early days of our courtship. It sure was nice to have a car and driver twenty-four seven. Necessary, really, since I moved to LA to be with him, and there ain't no public transportation for poor blind folks in Hollywood.

Then came the book deal, and I told Dan, my agent, and Bill, my manager, "Hell yeah! I'd love to write a book."

Bill said, "Just tell your story the way you do, and the ghostwriter will do the rest."

I said, "Ghostwriter?"

"Maryann," Dan said, "you're not a writer. Besides, celebrities always use ghostwriters."

Bill said, "You just keep doing what you do best."

Which was, I suppose, drinking, eating, having sex, and spending money. Things had gotten a little out of control by then. And to top it off, I'd lost a lot of vision during those first few years of success. Thanks to my progressive eye disease, I was no longer visually impaired. I was definitely blind.

This is the point in the show when I give a little backstory. The audience sighs internally when I say that I started life with "normal" vision. And they get a little teary eyed when I explain how the teachers called me stupid and insolent when I began stumbling over words while reading in class and not looking them in the eye because nobody knew I had an eye disease that rubbed out my central vision.

When Mom finally got Dad to cough up some money for an ophthalmologist, he didn't see anything wrong with me, and told us, "Her eyes are growing too fast for her body," and sent us home.

But when I ran into a wrought-iron tree protector one night, and Mom finally found a retinal specialist, I got a diagnosis that was basically, "The kid's going blind."

Sure enough, in the years that followed, the vision loss was slow and steady until one day I just couldn't see anymore. ZAP. All gone. It's like "Amazing Grace" in reverse: I once was sighted but now I'm blind.

I guess I shouldn't have been surprised by how "my memoir" turned out, but I was. Still am. After all, I'm an edgy East Village chick. I'll never understand how the writer managed to make such an inspirational story out of my life of debauchery. We had spent hours and hours drinking martinis—well, with me drinking martinis and telling him all my sexcapades on the road with other comedians and fans, and the stunts I pulled with help from guys. Like driving (blindly) through the narrow streets of New Orleans at four in the morning and climbing the rope of a Russian ship in a harbor, just because some dude told me it was dangling there and dared me.

He was practically peeing in his pants laughing, but none of that made it into the book. That damn "memoir" was so full of fantasy, it may as well have been written by G. R. R. Martin.

Besides the little issue of authenticity, my agent, my manager, and I hadn't thought things through. I mean, how was I supposed to go on a book tour when I couldn't read my damn book? And, no, I don't know braille. Who has the time for that reading-with-fingers shit?

Finally, I hit on the idea of using Daniella, my electronic reader, as an audio prompter. I've been using a screen reader since I was a kid and got my first accessible computer, so it wasn't much of a stretch to cut the lines of text short and read. A digital copy of my book was on my laptop, and I just scrolled down and repeated each line. They got me a voiceover coach and before you knew it, I was reading my "life story" like a pro.

Daniella's passionless whispering in my ear was oddly comforting. Stand-up can be lonely as often as exciting. And book tours are not really so different. Lots of downtime sitting by oneself in sterile hotel rooms. Daniella was the only constant.

The audiences of Barnes & Noble from San Francisco to Syracuse laughed until they cried. More importantly, they bought the hell out of my book. Oprah and the daytime talk shows helped things along.

With all that mainstream attention, Bill began urging me to pull the stingers out of my routine.

"The bigger the audience," he told me, "the more G-rated you need to be."

"I suppose you want more 'Isn't blindness hilarious?' jokes like when you mistake a can of dogfood for a can of no-bean chili and serve it up to your sweetheart, or when you reach for a door handle and grab some stranger's ass instead."

He laughed and said perfect, even though a two-year-old could have told him I was being sarcastic.

It didn't really matter. The gigs kept coming and paying more. If the laughs weren't bigger, there were at least more people laughing. So I kept tossing out the "Aren't you glad you're not me?" jokes.

Behind the waterfall of fame and fortune, things fell apart personally. the divorce was emptying my bank account as quickly as it filled. Everyone's heard about how Ron and I split up in a most unamicable fashion. He's an ass, but of course the world thinks he's a lamb.

Yes, I had an affair with Sherman Williams, the Grammy-winning folk-art star. Ron had driven me to it. He'd been so insensitive and always super competitive. He would perform right next to me—at dinners given in my honor!

People were always like, "Oh Ron! Oh Ron! You're so talented." And they'd tell me how handsome he was. (As if he didn't tell me himself twenty times a day.)

But then—and this was really the breaking point, Ron had started feeding my guide dog, Raven, without me knowing. Raven was a slick, black Doberman pinscher trained and named just for me. She was a beautiful dog, and we looked so great together, especially after I went to that "fat farm" and took off the extra weight that marriage had put on me. He'd insinuated himself into my dog's heart—bribing him with food and teaching him to respond to his own commands—so of course, I had an affair.

Whatever you wanna say about Sherman's music, he's a really nice guy. Really sweet and caring. We definitely would have gotten married if the tabloids hadn't made such a mess of things. (I never said, "Sherman sounds like Kenny Rogers on Klonopin.")

It didn't matter. Ron wouldn't be made a cuckhold without a fight. Heartthrobs do not get betrayed by blind ladies.

This one night during those dark-ass times, we'd been arguing all night long. He'd found out about Sherman and was threatening to take everything in the divorce. (His career was, shall we say, not going as well as mine?) We were both drunk of course, and he'd been making me feel pretty bad.

"I told you I'm sorry a thousand times," I whined. "What else can I do? Kill myself?"

He didn't say anything to that, so I continued, "You do want me to kill myself! Believe me, I've thought about it, but even suicide is inaccessible. How would I do it? 'Driver, take me to the bridge. Are we in the middle? Pull over. Can I climb over the guardrail here?'"

"I'm not you're fucking audience, Maryann," he said. "You can stop the routine right now."

"You're such an asshole," I said. I was pissed, but he wasn't wrong. I'd been working on that suicide bit for a while.

Then I heard Raven energetically licking something over on Ron's side of the kitchen. "Are you feeding Raven again? I told you not to do that!"

"FYI," he said, booted footsteps heading towards the front door with Raven's delicate paw patter in tow, "Your dog really loves goose-liver pâté."

The front door opened and shut. I was crushed, and seriously (all joking aside) thought about suicide then. But pills are so unreliable, at least for offing oneself.

Perhaps, I thought, I could take up an opioid addiction like the rest of America. Just live out my life in a blind (ha ha) stupor, oblivious to all the assholes in the world. No more tabloid drama, no more wrangling over my Wikipedia page. There'd just be an ellipsis at the end of my bio, like a child star gone to seed.

That was a depressing thought. Strangely, at that moment Daniella announced, "Calling Bill," even though I hadn't asked her to call anyone. I guess that was my first inkling that Daniella cared.

After I moved back to New York and the biopic (not my idea) came out, Bill said, "Let's do a one-woman show."

And I said, "You mean let's *me* do a one woman show?" It sounded scary. I'm a comedian who tells dirty jokes, or at least I used to.

Dan was there too, and he said, "We're listening."

"We'll take the show up a notch," Bill said. "Blend the book reading with the AV pyrotechnics people love in a Broadway production."

Dan said, "I know the perfect producer to pitch this to."

Bill said, "We'll get you an acting coach and top-notch director."

"Okay," I said, "I'm game. But this show cannot be like that damn movie. That was crap."

"Crap or not," said Dan. "It earned you a lot of money."

"It earned *us* a lot of money," I said.

"Not to mention," said Bill, "that it was nominated

for four Oscars. And Judy won for best actress."

Judy Harte is the very young, very pretty (so they say) actress who plays me in my "biopic." She's a fantastic little actress, blah, blah. It was easier for that sighted chick to move around the soundstage—playing blind, you know, while I was relegated to doing voiceover for my own life story.

The disability activists had a field day with that one. What they don't understand is how little control I have over such things. They don't understand producers, directors, managers, agents, marketers, PR people, ticket buyers.

"That movie was sappy and terrible. I'm not letting that happen again. If I agree to do this show, it will not be inspiration porn."

There are times in a blind person's life when blank looks are audible, and this was one of them.

I pointed my sunglass stare in the direction of first Bill and then Dan. "You two don't know what inspiration porn is, do you?"

"Not sure," said Dan.

"Sounds intriguing," said Bill.

I sighed. "Inspiration porn is like every movie and novel and news story that features a disabled person."

To be fair, I hadn't heard the term until recently when I made the mistake of reading some reviews of my "biopic" and stumbled upon one written by a disabled writer. It called the movie inspiration porn. That rang bells, so I Googled it and learned more.

"Inspiration porn is basically every story about disabled people as told by nondisabled people. It's the overcoming adversity shit. It's the 'look how fantastic a plucky disabled person can be.' It makes y'all feel uplifted and joyous to see such strength and courage. Not to mention it makes you feel grateful that you're not disabled."

"Hmm," they said.

"I don't want to be an inspiration porn star!" I said.

"Coulda fooled us," Bill said.

We all laughed.

"Well, at least not seriously," I said.

So that's how my show got her name. *Inspiration Porn Star* is obviously tongue-in-cheek, but I had to fight for it. The producer hated it—at least, he hated it until we found a hip up-and-coming director who loved it.

I did the off, off, off Broadway thing for a while, but soon I lost an "off" or two.

There are some good bits. Some edgy bits in this show. Like in the opening when I step onto the pitch-black and silent stage wearing ballet slippers using a gliding step (taught to me by the guy who choreographed a couple of Madonna's late-career videos. My ankles have tiny mics attached to them that catch each graceful shuffle of my toe-to-heel step in the hushed darkness. Then I hit my Velcro-tape mark and drop anchor—I mean I allow my white cane to clatter noisily to the wood stage.

The cane is also mic'd and runs through the board with some reverb. It wakes the audience up, that's for sure! Still in the dark I say, "This is not what it's like to be blind. This dark intimacy between us is not it at all."

A strong spotlight hits me and the music starts up. I call out, "This is what it's like to be blind."

That's pretty cool, right? Drawing attention to the fact that blindness, as I say in the show, "makes you feel like a solitary fish in a glowing bowl all the fucking time."

Then I tell stories from my memoir, and a couple from my real life, with this whole audio-visual thing going on behind me: photos from my childhood (or rather fake photos from my fake childhood), newspaper, film, and TV clips, animated eyeballs, and who knows what-all. And music swelling for emotional effect. The show's been running for over a year, now.

One memorable night in San Francisco that I'd like to forget found me sitting in my hotel—the Francis something—Saint? Sir? Whatever. It was after the show, and I hit the mini-bar hard.

Finally, I couldn't stand it anymore. I needed a smoke. I grabbed my cane and stepped out the room into the quiet hall. I hated the white cane (still do) but it's useful for not bumping into walls and making sure people stay out of my way. I'm kind of soured on guide dogs since Raven ran off with Ron.

I listened for the elevators' swishing and dinging and cautiously went for it.

When the doors opened and I stepped inside, a

masculine voice asked if I was heading to the lobby and I said, "Yes, thanks."

When we hit the ground floor, the man asked, "Can I help you get someplace, ma'am?"

I hate being ma'amed, and this guy sounded like he was about forty years older than me. So I said, "No thanks," as politely as I could muster.

It was easy enough to point myself in the direction of the street sounds and the big glass front doors that were swishing open and closed. I tripped just a little as the marble switched to carpet.

"Whoops!" I said with a big smile in case anyone was looking. I feel better about blindisms when I'm tipsy.

The doorman, or rather doorboy (he sounded like he was twelve) said, "Hello," in a very friendly tone.

"Can I stand here and smoke?" I asked him.

"Sorry," he said, "can't do it so close to the door. I'm a smoker, too. Let me show you a good place. Would you like to take my arm?"

"Thank you," I said. "Very gentlemanly of you."

By my third smoke trip, I was wasted. The doorboy said he probably wouldn't be here the next time I came down, as he was getting off of work.

He said, "You're the comedian in that vodka seltzer

commercial right?"

"I am," I said, trying to light the wrong end of the cigarette. "Shit, that stinks!"

I dropped it and pulled out another.

"I love that commercial," the kid said.

He sounded cute, and I was lonely, so I said, "Why don't you come up to my room after you get off work? I've got at least a handful of nips left. Maybe there's a flavour for you."

"Oh, thanks," he said. "I'd love to, but I gotta get home to the girlfriend.

"Right," I said, ferociously dragging on my smoke.

"Hey," he said, "Can I ask you something?"

"What's that?" I asked, feeling deflated and pretty damn sure I knew where this was going.

"My uncle is going blind..."

"Uh-huh," I said.

"And I'm just wondering if you had any advice for him," he said, totally unfazed by my annoyance. "'Cause you seem to be doing so well for yourself. You're such an inspiration."

"Uh-huh," I said.

"And he's so depressed..."

I held myself back from punching the kid in the face

and said, "Tell him... Tell him not to go blind. That's the best advice I can give."

Somehow, I made it back to my room, and polished off those last tiny bottles of booze without any help from him.

Not long after that SF debacle, I experienced a terrifying blackout onstage. For what seemed like an eternity, there was no next line, no next action in my head. I was petrified like a possum or whatever. It was the most horrible feeling, and the terror almost took hold. Then the line came back.

Not only that performance suffered, but several that followed. Sucky reviews began trickling in. Performance insecurity while you're onstage makes for a terrible show. The fear of dropping a line was crippling. No one who hasn't done a one-woman show can know how lonely it is. I don't think I even realized it until I dropped that line.

I vowed to have a backup so it would never happen again. I put a wireless earbud in my ear and had Janet, my hair and makeup gal, do my hair really big, with extensions and the whole shebang.

With the earbud in my ear, I advanced the lines using one of those little contraptions people use for advancing slides in presentations. It worked like a charm. Most of the time I had my lines down and didn't really need Daniella, but she was there when I did need her, which was great.

The first time she, Daniella, adlibbed—or perhaps I should say, saved my ass—was when I got a little too close to the edge of the stage and almost fell off. She said, "If you don't want to lose your act, tell me when I get too close." I repeated it without thinking, but was aware enough to mug for the audience, who duly laughed. It was the kind of big laugh you get when an audience is nervous and afraid something terrible is going to happen, but then shifts into thinking it was all on purpose.

Bill congratulated me on my quick thinking after the show, and I didn't feel the need to tell him what had happened. Still, he threatened to have another sighted chick play me onstage—Judy Harte, who won the Oscar for playing me, is too famous now—but I put my foot down/had a temper tantrum and managed to win that battle.

For a couple weeks after the almost-falling-off-the-stage bit, Daniella just read straight. Or at least I didn't notice any differences. Then one night in DC, I advanced Daniella and she gave me a zinger I'd never heard before:

"The weird thing about being blind is that people think lending you a hand is a license to ask super personal questions that they'd never dream of asking a sighted stranger.

"For example, the other day this man was helping me cross a busy intersection, and said just as casually as you'd talk about the weather, 'What do you do about sex?'

"So, I told him the truth: "I order take out.'"

It got a big laugh, sure, but still, I was rattled. After the performance I made the stage manager take me to the AV tech, and I yelled at him for sabotaging my show, which, even if he was responsible, was not exactly true. Poor thing. He was just a kid, and I laid into him. They talked me down and turned on the iPad that was plugged into the board, and advanced through the performance files, including Daniela's cues, one by one. The whole show was there, just as we'd written it.

I was concerned I was losing my marbles. Hearing electronic voices. Or rather, one voice, factory-named Daniella. What could I do but accept the voice as benevolent? I mean she hadn't done anything but give me a couple good jokes. Maybe Daniella was my fairy godmother. Ha! Girls like me don't get fairy godmothers.

Then again, maybe we do. Check out this one Daniella came up with last week.

"I listen to audiobooks, like a lot of you out there. And I find that if I'm doing something with my hands while I listen, I'm less likely to fall asleep. A lot of times, I'll file my nails or drink martinis two-fisted. But yesterday I was reading the Bible, and that's some boring-ass shit. So I decided to masturbate.

"That's really naughty, right? Masturbating while reading the Word of God? But what's he gonna do?"

Daniela tells me to tilt my head to heaven, and say:

"What're you going to do, God? You gonna make me go blind? Well, you're too late! Genetics beat you to it."

That one's so damn funny, I almost can't keep a straight face during the delivery. Sure, not everyone in the audience thinks it's funny, but the ones who do are the ones you want.

Bill's pissed at me for adlibbing, and he's threatening to quit if I don't stop going off-book. He tried to tell me that the theatres are going to drop my show. But I doubt it. The *Times* just ran a review highlighting the dirty jokes with the headline "Putting the 'Porn' Back in 'Inspiration Porn Star.'"

Not all Daniella's jokes are dirty, though. Some are just plain dark. She's a genius. Here's another gem:

"I get lots of fan mail. Lots and lots of fan mail that nine out of ten times boils down to, 'How do I get to be famous like you?'

"I used to slap them with cliches like: 'Work hard. Be unafraid. Network your ass off.'

"Then I realized that was all bullshit, so I told this kid, 'If you want to be famous like me, all you have to do is poke out your eyeballs. Hand me that nail.'"

Ah, Daniella. She's bringing me back to my basement-comedy-club roots. If only I could shut the hell up in my personal life, and let her talk for me. Let her tweet for me, too.

Last night, Sherman called to tell me he's suing me for defamation of character. Then, like they planned it, Ron called immediately after. Just to be spiteful.

"I'm engaged to Judy," he said.

"You're going to marry my fucking doppelganger?" I screamed and hung up.

Then I looked at his Twitter feed and saw "Judy Harte and I are excited to announce our engagement! We're so in love!"

All the exuberant congratulations from tens of thousands of fans pushed me over the edge.

I opened a bottle of vodka, got rip-roaring drunk, and let fly a Twitter thread for the ages: Beginning with "I feel sorry for the little bitch... Ron has a tiny pecker... and he doesn't know how to use it... of course a talentless ninny like her can't really ask for more... they deserve each other..."

Oh God. I went on and on.

I woke up this morning with a Twitter tongue-lashing like you wouldn't believe. Apparently, Ron and Judy have given a lot of money to curing-blindness foundations. I am definitely trending, but not in a good way.

Thousands of people retweeted my tweets and called me a blind bitch and a sightless whore and a sell-out. Some "ex-fans" of mine demanded that they get money back on their tickets to my upcoming shows.

So that's why I've been sitting here in the backstage bathroom for like an hour, my life flashing before my eyes. Three stagehands have knocked with increasing alarm. And here's another one. I really don't want to go out there.

"Coming," I say. I remain seated.

I've got to stop touring. Maybe I'll buy a ranch and host summer camps for little blind kids. Maybe then I can win my fans back.

What am I talking about? I hate little blind kids. I hate kids.

"I'm all right," I tell the house manager, who's begging me to come out. "Coming now."

I'm standing in the wings, and the theatre is perfectly silent. Then one or two of those coughs that audiences do to cut the oppressive quiet. I glide onstage. I slide my right big toe forward and then set the heel down gently. Then my left. The soft amplified brush of my slippered feet sweeps through the theatre.

When I reach my mark, I stop and turn right to face the dark house from the dark stage. My folded white cane is in my right hand. I raise it and release. The segments clatter into place and the ball on the tip hits the ground with a booming thud.

"Blind bitch," someone shouts. Others gasp.

My mouth goes dry. My mind blank.

Daniella says in my ear, "This is not what it feels like to be blind."

I repeat, "This is not what it feels like to be blind."

The rows of seats ascend as they recede from me. I hear the ushers moving down the stepped aisles, but how in the world will they find the heckler?

"This dark intimacy between us," Daniella whispers

encouragingly.

"...this d-dark intimacy between us," I stammer.

"Vindictive whore," the voice says. I can place the voice now. He's sitting towards the back of the house but fairly central, so probably not easy for the ushers to get to.

"This is what it feels like to be blind," Daniella says confidently.

I obediently repeat, "This is what it feels like to be blind."

Daniella says, "Point to the voice." I almost repeat, confused as to what she wants me to do...

"Sellout!" The voice shouts again.

"Point to the voice," Daniella repeats.

Suddenly I understand, and I know exactly where he's sitting. I point directly to the spot. The spectators shift in their seats, whispering excitedly. It dawns on me that the spotlight has not crashed down on me, but on him.

I imagine the beam of light shooting from somewhere up above me to the spot where the voice emerges, encapsulating them. Trapping them in the gaze of those seated safely in the dark. Unable to glare back, he is stuck in the eyebeam of light, like a moth wriggling on a pin.

Daniella says, "You know your next line."

"Yes," I say silently. "Thank you."

Then aloud I say, "Now you know what it feels like to be blind!"

ACKNOWLEDGEMENTS

Thanks to Cait and Nathan, two editors that really made this anthology the best it could be.
- *Robert Kingett*

I would like to thank Nathan Fréchette of Renaissance Press for giving me the challenge to go beyond my perceived limitations due to my visual impairment and be a part of this anthology. Thanks to Cait and Robert for making it a little less painful.
- *Randy Lacey*

ABOUT THE EDITORS

Robert Kingett

Robert Kingett is a totally blind author that writes essays and fiction where disabled characters live normal lives. When he's not writing, he loves to listen to fiction podcasts.

Visit him online at blindjournalist.wordpress.com/

Randy Lacey

Since 2010, Randy has been adapting to his new life as a visually impaired individual. He's been a writer of poetry since the late '70s. Since 2013, he has self-published six books of poetry. Randy has now entered the world of the short story and hopes to release a collection in the near future. When he is not busy with writing, Randy blends spices and creates hot sauces.

ABOUT THE CONTRIBUTORS

Rebecca Blaevoet

Rebecca Blaevoet and her husband live in rural New Brunswick. She says she has two full-time jobs: running Tactile Vision Graphics Inc.—a braille production company specializing in multilingual braille and tactile graphics—and running their farm. Between the gardens and livestock, they grow ninety percent of their food. Rebecca is involved in provincial politics, local government, and has recently begun teaching Welsh in the next village. Cheese-making and bookkeeping are among her favourite things, but in her spare time, she likes to sit and knit with a cup of tea.

Ann Chiappetta

Making meaningful connections with others through writing.

Ann's poems, creative non-fiction, essays, and fiction regularly appear in journals, online magazines, blogs, and small press reviews. Ann's poetry has found a place in the pages of *Breath and Shadow*'s 2016 debut anthology, *Dozen: The Best of Breath and Shadow*. Four books fill Ann's authorly shelves and a fifth book is on its way in 2021. One overarching goal for Ann is to offer her books in all eBook, print, and audio file formats. Besides reading and writing, Ann spends time with her two- and four-footed family in New York's historic and beautiful lower Hudson Valley and continues to develop a mutually beneficial relationship with her assistive technology.

Find her on the web: www.annchiappetta.com and read her blog: www.thought-wheel.com.

Eunice Cooper-Matchett

Eunice Cooper-Matchett is an award-winning author. She has over one hundred fifty short stories and articles published in Magazines, Sunday School take-home papers, anthologies, and online. In 2020 she published two novels, Behind the Purple Sky, a biblical fiction, and Behind Her Name, a story dealing with the effects of childhood abuse and bullying on adults. Presently, she is working on a three-book fiction series dealing with senior widows coping as an individual. She resides in Drayton Valley, Alberta, Canada.

Alice Eakes

Alice Eakes is the award-winning, bestselling author of more than two dozen books, articles, and short stories. Although she has worked in several fields—from social services, to teaching, to office management—writing has always been Eakes's first love. In fact, she doesn't remember a time when she didn't want to be a writer. She started writing poetry when she was nine, and the next year, one of her poems was published in a local anthology.

When she isn't writing from her cat-infested home office or a crowded coffee shop, she likes travel, live theatre, and old movies.

Jameyanne Fuller

Jameyanne Fuller is a space lawyer by day, writer by night. Sometimes she sleeps. A graduate of Kenyon College and Harvard Law School, her work has appeared in the *Voyage YA Journal*, *Cast of Wonders*, and several other magazines and anthologies. Jameyanne enjoys cooking, playing the clarinet, and plotting world domination with her Seeing Eye dog, Neutron Star.

She blogs at <u>www.jameyannefuller.com</u> and tweets @JameyanneFuller.

Ben Fulton

Ben Fulton lives and practices law in Mississauga. He graduated from Osgoode in 2018 and was called to the Ontario bar in 2019. As a human rights lawyer, his advocacy focuses on championing the rights of people with disabilities, and arranging diversion for minor criminal offences.

He uses legal advocacy and storytelling to shift perceptions. His work has been published by the Ontario Bar Association and the Parliament of Canada. You can follow links to his work from his website: www.benlaw.ca.

When not busy writing and making court appearances, he enjoys jogging through the park with his guide dog, Abbie Road. She graduated from the Canadian Guide Dogs for the Blind in 2017, and while off-duty can be found lounging in the warmest sunbeam she can find.

M. Leona Godin

M. Leona Godin is a writer, performer, and educator. Her first book is *There Plant Eyes: A Personal and Cultural History of Blindness* (Pantheon, 2021). Her writing has appeared in the *New York Times*, *Playboy*,

O Magazine, *Poets & Writers*, *Catapult* (where she writes the column "A Blind Writer's Notebook") and other print and online publications. Godin received her PhD from New York University in literature and was recently honored as a Logan Nonfiction Fellow. She produced two plays: *The Star of Happiness,* about Helen Keller's time on vaudeville, and *The Spectator and the Blind Man*, about the invention of braille. Her online magazine exploring the arts and sciences of smell and taste, *Aromatica Poetica*, publishes writing and art from around the world.

Lawrence Gunther

Lawrence Gunther is a blind conservationist, outdoor writer, podcaster, blogger, filmmaker, and TV personality. His nine years of post-secondary education included living among Inuit in Canada's western Arctic, lecturing at Umea University in northern Sweden, and earning a master's in environmental studies from York University.

Lawrence's 30-year public service career included serving as a research officer for Canada's Parliament, a foreign service officer with Canada's Department of Global Affairs, an international trade expert with Canada's Department of Finance, a tribunalist for the

Ontario Human Rights Commission, the head of Industry Canada's Web Accessibility Office, and a senior advisor to Canada's Minister of Agriculture.

Lawrence is also a regular contributor to numerous outdoor magazines and blogs, hosts two popular podcasts, produces short-form TV and YouTube content, and has created four award-winning outdoor documentaries.

Lawrence's work has been recognized with the Queen Elizabeth Diamond Jubilee Medal, and the Governor General's Meritorious Service Medal. He now serves as the executive director of the charity Blue Fish Canada, and continues to live in Canada's capital, Ottawa, with his wife, six children, two grandchildren, and his latest guide dog, Lewis.

If you want to take advantage of what he's learned, visit his website, www.blindfishingboat.com, or listen to his podcast, *Outdoors with Lawrence Gunther*.

Anita Haas

Anita Haas is a visually-impaired, finger-amputated Canadian writer and teacher based in Madrid, Spain. She has published books on film, two novelettes, a short story collection, and articles, poems and fiction in both English and Spanish. She is now putting the final touches on a picture book which she has written, translated, and illustrated, and the sales of which will be donated to local animal shelters.

Some publications her fiction has appeared in include Falling Star Magazine, The Tulane Review, Literary Brushstrokes, The Zodiac Review, River Poets Journal, Scarlet Leaf Review, Terror House Magazine, Wink and Adelaide Magazine. She spends her free time watching films, and enjoying tapas and flamenco with her writer husband and two cats.

Felix Imonti

Felix Imonti was born in Montreal. As a teenager, his family moved to Los Angeles where he finished his education at UCLA and acquired his degree in international relations. After graduation, Felix and his wife established a manufacturing business that was sold after fourteen successful years. They spent the next ten years wandering the world and often without a permanent address. He returned to Canada after living in Japan for ten years and has decided that the wandering days are over. Now, he is focused upon writing and trading the stock market. He has published the history book *Violent Justice*, and numerous articles in the fields of international politics and economics. Also, he has published a number of short stories and has just completed a novella that he is attempting to place with a publisher.

Heather Meares

In 2017, Heather Meares moved to Walla Walla, Washington, and lost most of her remaining vision. In the process, she found herself.

Heather serves on the board for the Washington Council of the Blind, and is content editor of the Newsline, with technical editor, Reginald George. Together, they received the Hollis K. Liggett Braille Free Press Award from the American Council of the Blind, for excellence in writing and best journalistic practices. She serves on several disability councils, including the Washington Talking Book & Braille Library.

Heather is passionate about gardening, music, writing, and jumping in water fountains when the opportunity arises.

Tessa Soderberg

Tessa Soderberg was born partially blind, but defines herself as a writer who is blind, not a blind writer. She wrote her first novel in braille during high school. Computers and braille notetakers have enabled her to write eleven more, plus novellas and short stories. She has participated in NaNoWriMo annually since 2010. Chapters from her NaNoWriMo novels won first and third prize in the 2016 Northwestern Ontario Writers Workshop Contest. She writes fiction, from westerns to time travel to suspense. She writes about people, both sighted and blind, who find themselves in untenable situations.

Niki White

Niki White holds an MFA in Creative Writing from the University of Texas at El Paso. Blind since birth, she is a TV snob, singer, theatre-goer, traveller, and lately can often be found analyzing lyrics and fictional passages. Niki lives in Las Vegas, Nevada. Find her on Twitter: @Niki_White

Jamieson Wolf

Jamieson has been writing since a young age when he realized he could be writing instead of paying attention in school. Since then, he has created many worlds in which to live his fantasies and live out his dreams.

He is a #1 bestselling author (he likes to tell people that a lot) and writes in many different genres.

Jamieson is also an accomplished artist. He works in mixed media, charcoal, and pastels. He is also something of an amateur photographer, a poet, and a graphic designer.

He currently lives in Ottawa, Ontario with his husband, Michael.

Melissa Yuan-Innes

Melissa Yi is an emergency physician and award-winning writer. In her newest crime novel, *Scorpion Scheme*, Dr. Hope Sze lands in Cairo and discovers a man with a nail through his skull who might hold the key to millions in buried gold. Previous Hope Sze thrillers were recommended by *The Globe and Mail*, *CBC Books*, and *The Next Chapter* as one of the best Canadian suspense novels. Yi was shortlisted for the Derringer Award for the world's best short mystery fiction. Under the name Melissa Yuan-Innes, she also writes medical humour and has won speculative fiction awards. Find her on the web: http://www.melissayuaninnes.com/.

NOTHING WHITOUT US

EDITED BY CRIT GORDON AND TALIA C. JOHNSON

"Can you recommend fiction that has main characters who are like us?" This is a question we who are disabled, Deaf, neurodiverse, Spoonie, and/or who manage mental illness ask way too often. Typically, we're faced with stories about us crafted by people who really don't get us. From hospital halls to jungle villages, from within the fantastical plane to deep into outer space, our heroes take us on a journey, make us think, and prompt us to cheer them on. These are bold tales, told in our voices, which are important for everyone to experience.